It Came Upon a Midnight Crime

A Squeaky Clean Novella
Book 2.5

By Christy Barritt

IT CAME UPON A MIDNIGHT CRIME

A special thanks to Kathy Applebee and Janet Musgrove for your help, support, and encouragement with this book!

Chapter 1

Twas the Crime Before Christmas

"I clean up blood and guts. Not plastic dead people," I mumbled into the phone as I bounced down the highway in my van.

"Please, Gabby." Pastor Shaggy's voice cracked in earnest. "Could you just swing by and take a look? The lady is down on her luck. She hurt her foot and can barely walk. She could really use a hand. I'd help her myself, but I have meetings lined up all day."

The last thing I needed was to do a job for free—especially since I had bills piling up. But how could I say no to a man of God? Would lightning strike me if I did? Or perhaps plagues would descend my apartment or I'd be swallowed by a big fish and remain in his belly until I changed my mind? I couldn't be sure. Pastor Shaggy had been there for me before, like when I needed someone to do a eulogy for a reclusive stranger with no family. I couldn't say that about very many people.

I tapped my finger on the steering wheel,

considering my options. "Fine, but only because I'm just down the road. Otherwise, I'd say no because my schedule is entirely too packed."

If only that were true. I was practically begging people to give me jobs so I could pay my bills. Usually, Christmastime was hopping with jobs for my crime scene cleaning business. Crooks must be in the holiday spirit this year and trying to make it onto Santa's "Nice" list.

"You're the best, Gabby. Super awesome."

"I know." I smiled, hung up and tossed my phone into my purse beside me.

"What was that about?" Chad, my business partner, pulled off one of his candy cane striped socks and examined a hangnail. Gross. But that was Chad for you. He was cute if you liked the surfer type who delighted in toe jam.

"I'll let you see firsthand."

We pulled up to the crime scene, which was really a Cape Cod house located in an older neighborhood with more spacious yards than most. A huge life-sized nativity had once been set up, based on what I saw now, all across the front yard. A police car, an unmarked sedan, and a practical compact were in the driveway.

A practical compact? If I looked inside, I bet I'd find the floorboards absent of even a blade of dried grass or a gum wrapper. Was that Riley's car?

What was he doing here?

My throat burned as I got out of my unmarked white van with the jostling cleaning equipment in the back. My feet crunched across the dry grass until I reached the hoard of people gathered around a homemade nativity. Sure enough, there beside Pastor Shaggy was Riley Thomas, a man with a heart that even Mother Teresa would admire—except when it came to dating.

I marched up to Riley and put my hands on my hips, trying to ease into the confusion.

"What are you doing here?" Yep, I had a way with words. I had a way with blurting them out like a redneck spit tobacco. Luckily, my friends still loved me.

Riley, an attorney who was also known as Mr. Tall, Dark and Handsome, looked down at me, those baby blue eyes as perceptive and warm as ever. "Good to see you too, Gabby."

I pushed a red curl out of my face before staring him in the eye. "Fill me in."

He nodded toward the distance. "The owner of this house makes life-sized nativity figures out of chicken wire. She adds to her collection every year, and a lot of locals make it a point to drive out here and look at them annually. Last night, someone ran over the figures. Best we can tell, they're all flattened."

I looked in the background and saw a thin middle-aged Asian woman hobbling painfully on crutches with tears—and gobs of mascara—running down her face. All of that hard work destroyed. I'd cry, too.

All of the life-size figures were now on the ground, almost reminding me of a police reconstruction scene of a shooting. I closed my eyes for a moment and visualized what the scene must have looked like before being demolished. There were clothes, wigs, hay bales, and various other items scattered all over the yard.

I stared back at Riley. "And you're here why?"

"I've been consulting with the pastor just in case someone wants to go the legal route. We're not there yet, but we're trying to be diligent."

"The legal route?" I looked around me. This was a prank, if anything. I didn't see the dismembered Mary and Joseph needing a lawyer so they could head to court any time soon.

"Someone's trying to get a very specific point across. In return, some of these victims could press charges in an effort to send a proactive message that this is not acceptable. We think these vandalisms tie in with a couple of other cases I'm involved with right now."

I shoved my hands into my pockets. "I can't

argue with that." My gaze scanned the area as a brisk wind swept over the lawn. The skin on my face tightened. "Anything else strange about the scene?"

"We're still looking at everything." Detective Adams appeared, his hair disheveled and his eyes sagging like he'd been working too much. The man was in his fifties, stocky and bald, and about as much of a fixture around the Norfolk P.D. as police car sirens. "Ms. St. Claire. Why am I not surprised to see you here?"

"I'm going to help clean the scene as soon as it's released."

Riley stepped forward. "And that's where her involvement ends."

My eyebrows came together as I scowled. "Pastor Shaggy called me here to help." I pointed across the yard to the pastor. His name wasn't really Shaggy, but he looked just like the character from the Scooby Doo cartoon. He was lanky and tall with a scraggly voice, but man could he ever preach a mean sermon.

"To help clean up," Riley clarified.

Before I had time to argue, Chad yelled from across the yard. "Guys, you might want to see this." He squatted by one of the figures lying in the grass. Joseph maybe? It was hard to tell.

We all circled around him as he stared down

at the figure's face. His expression held a twist of excitement and dread when he looked up at us. He pointed with a stick to Joseph's head. "This is hair."

"We can see that." Detective Adams twisted his lips in annoyance.

Chad shook his head. "No, this is human hair. The scalp is still attached."

Chapter 2

The Most Wonderful Crime of the Year

"Why would someone leave human hair? Did they murder someone?" It didn't matter that I worked crime scenes for a living. The idea of murder still made my blood go Frosty-the-Snowman cold.

Chad would know about human hair and the like. He was a mortician before deciding life was too short to do a job you hated. He took up giving ski lessons and being a whitewater rafting guide for a while. Then he came to Virginia Beach to surf and to start a crime scene cleaning business. We'd been rivals for a while before we decided we were stronger if we worked together.

So far, so good. Our partnership had only been intact for a couple of months now. It did feel good to have someone help to carry the workload. It didn't feel good to have to split my paycheck.

Suddenly, Detective Adams seemed interested—way interested—in this case. That's right. The criminal had just proven they weren't wearing kid gloves. No, this was the real deal. "This investigation has just ratcheted up a few notches," Detective Adams mumbled as he kneeled beside the flattened figure.

Riley looked at me, concern filling his eyes. "You need to stay away from this, Gabby."

I narrowed my eyes at him. He'd mentioned that a few times already. "Why?"

"Because, as always, danger seems to be following you. Ten minutes ago, this whole case just seemed like someone trying to make a statement about Christmas. Now it's about murder, and I don't think you should be involved. I just want to state that for the record."

"I'll be fine."

"You say that a lot. You almost get killed a lot, also."

"Almost is the key word there. I'm still alive, aren't I?" Despite the lightheartedness of my words, I knew I wouldn't be alive if it wasn't for my friends. They'd gotten me out of more than one deep-fried pickle before.

"I just want you to be careful."

Aw, Riley *did* care about me, didn't he? No, I couldn't think like that. Thinking like that made me weak. I was not one of those women who waited around for a man to come to his senses and date her. Riley had his chance, and he blew it.

Would someone please tell my heart the

news?

I raised my hand in a pledge. "I will use the utmost caution and reason."

I couldn't stop the gleam from sparkling in my eyes. Before Riley could respond, I strode across the lawn toward the woman who owned the house. Sure enough, her foot was in a cast, which would make it more difficult to clean up this mess. My question was: Was her injury related to this case?

I extended my hand. "I'm Gabby St. Claire and I'm a crime scene—" I ran my hand over my mouth as I finished, "—cleaner."

Her hand continued to cover her mouth as she stared at the destruction around her. "I'm Arlene Matthews."

"Any idea why someone would do this?" I asked.

She sniffled. "No idea. It's just senseless."

"What if it's not? Did you make anyone angry?"

"No, no one." Her voice cracked as a new round of tears began.

"Are you sure?" She was my first and only lead as of now, so her noncommittal answers would not work.

She fluttered her hand in the air. "Look, the only person I can remotely think of that I've had an argument with was that woman from the costume shop."

"What costume shop?" Now we were getting somewhere.

"Chadwick's on 21st."

"What happened?"

"I tried to return one of the outfits I bought because it didn't work for my nativity figure. She came up with this crazy excuse as to why I couldn't get my money back. She's a Scrooge, I tell you. I threatened to report her to the Better Business Bureau and to call the local TV stations and tell them how horrible she was. I wouldn't have really done it, but I just wanted my money back. That costume was over one-hundred dollars!" She shook her head. "That lady was nasty, but I don't think she would have done this."

Interesting. I stored that information away in the back of my mind before pointing to her foot. "What happened?"

"Just a little fall from my front porch. Someone left these little plastic balls—they were so small they looked like salt pellets almost—all over my steps. I didn't see them in time."

"When did that happen?"

"Just a couple of days ago. Right after I set up my nativity scene, for that matter."

I nodded, taking mental notes, when from across the lawn I spotted Detective Adams storming toward me. I scooted out of the way before I got an earful, promising to come back and clean up for her when the scene was cleared.

I hurried back toward my van. As I walked, something wedged into a garden of azaleas caught my eye. I picked up a piece of paper and carefully unfolded it.

Handwritten words stared back at me.

The Most Wonderful Crime of the Year.

My heart raced.

It looked like I'd just found another clue.

***

The next day, a new excitement fluttered through me, and it wasn't just because I'd already downed four cups of coffee.

Last night, I'd hung around the crime scene for as long as I could, despite the fact that Detective Adams and Riley had tried numerous times to shoo me away. Nothing else had been discovered at Arlene's house, but now I had this insatiable curiosity and determination to figure out what had happened.

Someone had to help that poor woman who'd made the Holy Family out of chicken wire. Why not me? The scalp and the note had been the clincher. What kind of sick, twisted person would do something like that? Were they trying to send a message? Or did this go deeper—like, serial killer deeper?

I stood at my apartment door, listening to everything happening on the other side. I lived in an old Victorian that had been divided up into five little dwellings. Riley lived across the hall from me.

My ears perked when I heard his door opening.

Quickly, I grabbed my coat and rushed out to the second-floor landing, trying in vain to look casual. Riley's eyes widened in surprise when he saw me. "Gabby. You're up early."

I matched his stride as he went down the stairs. "Where are you going?"

"Why would you ask?"

I shrugged, trying to look innocent. "Did something else happen?"

"What are you talking about?" His voice was maddeningly calm and even.

I grabbed his arm. "You know what I'm talking about. I know you and the pastor have started this campaign to save Christmas, so anything that happens around town that's Christmas related—or anti-Christmas related— you're going to be there."

He frowned. "You're too smart for your own good sometimes, Gabby."

I nearly squealed. "So I'm right! What happened?"

He started walking again, letting out a little sigh as he did so. "I really don't think you should get involved. This is more than just some little pranks, and I don't want to see you get hurt."

I didn't want to resort to whining. I really didn't. But . . . "Oh, come on. I don't have anything better to do. And this is good experience. I'm going to be a forensic investigator one day. What better way to learn the ropes than to investigate on my own?"

He stared at me another moment before finally nodding. "Come on. But, for the record, I don't approve."

"And for the record, I hear you."

As I climbed into his car, I picked up a flyer that had been left on the front seat. The front read, Operation: Save Christmas. Pastor Shaggy had come up with a plan to revitalize the true meaning of Christmas throughout the area of Norfolk, Virginia. It consisted of several events around the city, like a Living Christmas Tree, that would keep the holidays focused on Jesus. I was sure Pastor Shaggy hoped it would eventually go viral and sweep the nation.

I was just coming to grips with this whole religion thing myself and I supposed the idea of "saving Christmas" sounded quaint and idealistic enough. I mean, was I totally on board? No. My science-loving self was way too analytical to accept that Jesus—the supposed Savior of the world—was born of a virgin and that he later conquered death in order to bring the human race life. But let people believe what they were going to believe. Let them hold onto the warmth and coziness of imagining angels singing "The First Noel" while a star lit the path for wise men and shepherds. The story had its appeal, as did Greek mythology for that matter. I had to admit that I liked the idea of someone giving their life for me—like Jesus supposedly did on the cross. I certainly couldn't imagine anyone actually doing that. Not for me, at least. Yet, Riley was smart and he believed in all of it. So what was my hang-up?

Ten minutes later, we were standing outside a historic church in Norfolk, Virginia. It was located in the heart of the bustling little downtown area and right across the street from My Dung, a cheap Chinese restaurant that made my stomach growl for some General Tso's chicken. The church grounds had once displayed what some might call a "handsome" nativity scene, but someone had put a quick end to that holiday marker by using some type of explosive device. Mary was now in the cemetery, Joseph had been blown to shreds, and Jesus was nowhere to be found.

I hurried toward Pastor Shaggy, pulling my coat tighter as another arctic blast swept across the lawn. "Any body parts found yet?"

Pastor Shaggy rubbed his scruffy chin while shaking his head before kicking a melted camel's head back toward the point of the explosion. "Not that I've been told."

"An eerie note?"

Shaggy nodded. "The pastor told me they found a note. It said, 'The Slaying Song.'"

"A play on words with 'The Sleighing Song.'" I shivered, not as much from the cold as from the cryptic message that had been left.

Across the lawn, the CSI team bent over a wise man. I excused myself and crept closer, hoping to overhear something—anything—that might let me know what was going on.

"Is that an ear?" I heard one of the investigators say.

An ear? I peered a little closer. Sure enough, it looked like someone had glued a human ear to the wise man. Sick, sick, sick.

"Ms. St. Claire!"

I nearly jumped out of my skin as Detective Adams came into focus. I cleared my throat and raised my chin. "Detective Adams."

"I thought I told you not to get involved."

"Define 'involved'."

He scowled. "You know precisely what I mean."

"Any missing people who might be connected with these body parts?"

His scowl deepened. "That's none of your business."

My gaze roamed behind him at the mess that church officials were just waiting for the okay to clean up. Several parishioners—I assumed that's who they were—wandered the grounds or talked in clusters. I was pretty sure from the way they kept looking over their shoulders that they thought this was the first sign of Armageddon or, at the very least, the end of life as they knew it.

I nodded toward ground zero, as if it were my business. "Hate crime?"

"I'd say it was just teenagers up to some mischief with a bottle bomb, if it wasn't for—" He stopped himself, but I knew what he was going to say, *If it wasn't for the ear.*

"I still think this should be considered a hate crime."

"I appreciate your opinion. As always." His voice did not match his words.

Yes, I did have a lot of opinions. I couldn't deny that. Riley said that was just the way that God had made me.

I turned away from the detective. There was

nothing more I could do here. I was not an explosive expert, not in the least—unless you counted the time I accidentally blew up the chemistry lab in high school. But that was an entirely different story.

Now, I had a promise to make good on.

***

Riley had given me a ride back to the apartment, where I'd grabbed my van and rode out to yesterday's crime scene. I'd promised I'd clean it—something I was regretting at the moment. I didn't mind working for free sometimes, but that was usually when I had money coming in from other sources, which I didn't right now.

I was hoping that I might discover something new today, but I hadn't. Mostly, I'd tried to pat the homeowner's back, tell her everything would be okay, and piece back together the nativity figures. I'd counted on being there maybe a couple of hours, but ended up being there nearly six.

Now it was time to unwind with my friends.

I climbed into my unmarked work van, and a few minutes later I pulled up to my favorite coffeehouse, The Grounds, which just so happened to be located right across from my apartment. The sun was already beginning to sink and the air felt crisp with winter. All along the road, fake boughs of holly had been shaped into twirls around light poles. I resisted the urge to mutter, "Ba-humbug!" I didn't have great memories of Christmas. My mom had mostly cried because my brother wasn't with us anymore, and my dad had gotten drunk. I spent much of the time feeling guilty that my brother was gone. There was absolutely nothing merry about any of that.

As I pulled open the door to The Grounds, the scent of cinnamon and coffee warmed me. "Run, Run Rudolph" played from the overhead speakers and made me want to put a little swing in my step, but before I could fully engage my jazz hands with the two-step, my friends waved me over from a corner table. I composed myself as I approached the table where Riley, Chad, and Sierra sat.

"What took so long?" Riley asked, pushing out a chair for me. "Everything okay?"

I plopped down suddenly weary. "Long story."

Riley shoved a vanilla latte in my hand. "You're going to have to drink this on the go, then."

"Where are we going?" I took a sip of my drink and noticed there was some cinnamon, nutmeg, and maybe even caramel in this latte. I just couldn't get away from the reminders that Christmas was approaching, could I? I mean, it wasn't that I really wanted to forget. It was mostly that when you're single and without a close family, Christmas isn't that exciting. Sure, my aunt would send me oversized granny underwear and my dad might spring for some cheap chocolates. Heck, he might even wrap up some of his bills and give them to me as a way of saying "Aren't you glad I'm your dad?" But Christmas . . . it was just another day, one I'd just as soon pass by.

"We're buying you a Christmas tree," Riley announced

I nearly spit out my latte. "What? I don't want a tree."

"Come on, Gabby. You've gotta have a tree," Sierra chimed in, pushing her plastic framed glasses up higher on her tiny little nose. "My Christmas won't be merry and bright if I think you're miserable."

"I'm not miserable." Okay, so maybe a little.

"We've developed a plan," Chad added. "The Christmas tree is first on the list. Then we're taking you to a Christmas parade and we're dragging you to the Ugly Christmas Sweater party at Sierra's."

"Guys, I have more important things to do. I've got to figure out who's destroying Christmas around town." That sounded more noble than being nosy, didn't it?

"I really don't think you should . . . " Riley

started.

I raised a hand. "I know. But I'm a big girl. And I'm not totally investigating. I'm just nosing around. You know, what I do best."

Sierra, a second-generation Japanese American and animal rights activist, stood to her full four-foot eleven-inch height. "Okay, enough arguing. We've got to concentrate on the mission at hand, and that mission involves visiting a tree stand run by Boy Scout Troop 14 and maybe admiring some Christmas lights along the way."

There was really no use in arguing. We left the coffee shop and padded down the sidewalk in Ghent, an artsy little neighborhood located in Norfolk, Virginia. Sierra and Chad bantered back and forth as we walked, arguing about whether reindeer could fly and, even if they could, how ethical it would be to force them to pull a sled. I tuned them out, walking in companionable silence beside Riley. My breath came out in frosty puffs and somewhere nearby—from Sierra maybe?—I could hear little jingle bells tinkling with each footfall.

"You find out anything today, Ms. I'm-Not-Investigating-Just-Being-Nosy?" Riley asked. He was tall and lean with a head full of dark hair that was just a little too long—his hair was probably the only part of him that ever rebelled. He had crystal blue eyes, a knock-your-socks-off grin, and I was convinced he was the secret twin of the guy who played the lead character on the TV show *Grimm*. I seriously needed for him to grow some warts, gain a ton of weight, and obtain some bad body odor. Then maybe he wouldn't be so endearing to me.

I shrugged. "Not really. Nothing good, at least."

His hands were shoved down into the pockets of his black leather coat. I wondered if Sierra had admonished him yet for wearing that jacket and therefore supporting animal cruelty—those would have been her words, not mine. I wasn't a fan of animal cruelty, but I was a fan of eating meat.

By the time we reached the tree stand, my latte was long gone and my hands were freezing. The makeshift business was located in the parking lot off to the side of a strip of upscale shops. I walked through the rows of trees, absorbing the scent of evergreens. Finally, I pointed to a tree nearly buried between some other behemoths. "I want that one."

Riley squinted at it. "That one?

I nodded most assuredly. "Yep, that one."

"It's . . . small and lopsided."

"Yep, and that's why I want it. No one else will."

His piercing blue eyes met mine, and I could

see in their depths that he was trying to understand me. Finally, he said, "Trees don't have feelings, you know. It's not going to spend all night crying because it was picked last."

Everyone had to be a smart aleck, didn't they? "I know. I just . . . I don't know. I feel a kindred spirit with it, I suppose. I know it sounds corny. I just know that I want this one."

Riley pulled it out from its hiding spot and stood it on end. The tree probably only came to my shoulders and about half of its branches were either missing or broken. Like I said, it was perfect.

Riley nodded. "It's a done deal then."

I paid for the tree and then Riley hoisted it over his shoulder. I was going to have to find some Christmas ornaments somewhere to decorate the pitiful little evergreen. I'd think about that later. Maybe I'd get creative and use some of the gag gifts people had gotten me throughout the years, things like bouncing balls that looked like eyes and crime scene tape. I'd bet I could get on Pinterest and find some ideas for making my old rubber work gloves into angels or something.

We stopped outside of my apartment building, and Sierra turned to all of us. "How about if I meet you guys up in Gabby's apartment? I want to grab some brownies from my place. I made them today."

I paused by the steps, remembering the last time Sierra made brownies for us. I had to think of a way to say no and fast. Or should I simply pretend to eat the brownie while secretly throwing the rest of it out of the window for the squirrels?

Just as I opened my mouth to speak, my gaze focused on a wooden manger scene Riley had placed outside of our building. It looked like someone had taken an ax to the set and chopped it up in pieces. My jaw dropped open. "No . . . "

Sierra's hands went to her hips. "What's wrong with my brownies?"

Riley followed my gaze. He walked over to the scene and bent down, shaking his head as he picked up a chunk of wood. "Why would someone do this?"

"That's a great question." It couldn't be a coincidence that someone had destroyed this manger scene. I joined Riley and knelt down to examine the destruction. I knew this meant a lot to him. "I'm sorry."

He shook his head again. "It's okay. I just don't understand . . . "

I pointed to the blanket under the manger. "Look, I think there's a piece of paper there."

Riley reached over and tugged at the corner. Sure enough, a note was there. He pulled his shirtsleeves over his fingers—careful not to damage any prints—and opened the paper. The message was simple—and eerie: *Away in a Danger.*

"Away in a Danger?" I questioned, trying to process everything aloud.

Riley shook his head. "Someone is sick."

I knew one thing. Someone had just sent me a personal invitation to get involved in this investigation.

And I was accepting.

Chapter 3

Mr. Grinch

The next morning, I pulled to a stop in front of a white-steepled church in downtown Norfolk. I was pretty sure this was one of the historic buildings that people always talked about with local pride. I had to admit that the place was gorgeous and picturesque with its white-planked sides, stained glass windows, and neat cemetery surrounded by a picket fence.

I put the van in park and glanced at my watch. Pastor Shaggy was holding a meeting for Operation: Save Christmas, and I wanted to be there and check out the crowd.

I yawned and rested my head against the seat. Seven o'clock still felt early to me. I'd had another late night since we'd called Detective Adams to the manger scene massacre at my apartment building. He'd offered no insight and had again warned me to leave this investigation to the authorities. What fun was that?

Finally, a few more cars pulled into the

parking lot and people straggled toward the front door. They looked like they needed coffee more than I did. When Pastor Shaggy arrived, that's when I decided to go inside. I put aside the piles of paperwork I'd been working on for my business.

He paused at the front door, and as the sunlight hit his hand, I noticed the scrape across the top. "I'm glad you could come, Gabby. This means a lot."

I wasn't sure he realized that I was here more for the crime part than I was the "save Christmas" part. "Someone made it personal, so I didn't have much of a choice." I softened my voice. "But I'm glad to help out."

I was about to ask about that cut on his hand, when someone else called him away to begin the meeting. Instead, I found a seat in the hard wooden pew located at the back of the room.

I looked around the sanctuary at the twenty or so people who'd gathered. There were all kinds of people there—all races, social statuses, and ages. All concerned citizens. Pastor Shaggy had told me there were teachers, preachers, chaplains, civic group leaders, and everyday people who wanted to make a difference.

And they all listened to Pastor Shaggy as he walked on stage and began talking about various Christmas events going on around town and what people's legal rights were. People nodded and listened and asked questions.

The whole scene was very inspiring, but it didn't give me any leads as to who might be behind the dastardly anti-Christmas deeds.

As people filed away and another hour of my life dwindled past, I approached Pastor Shaggy. Just as I was about to launch into my questions, a woman ran up to him. She was probably in her thirties, tall with an athletic build, and long brown hair.

"You were fabulous today, Pastor. I just wanted to let you know that."

I was pretty sure that Pastor Shaggy blushed. "Thanks, Charity." He glanced back over at me. "Charity, this is Gabby St. Claire. Charity is a high school chemistry teacher and also has been my right hand in trying to get everything organized here."

Charity offered a wide grin. "All of this talk about Christmas being banned just fired me up. I knew I had to get involved. For the children's sakes, mostly." She looked back at Pastor Shaggy. "We'll talk more about the Living Christmas Tree this afternoon. Is that okay? I've got to be at school in ten minutes."

"Sounds perfect, Charity."

As she trounced away, I looked back at

Pastor Shaggy. "You like her, don't you?"

He blushed. I promise he did. "No, don't be silly."

I shook my head, veering way too far off topic. "Okay, let's cut all the politically correct niceties out. Who do you think would do this?"

He raised his eyebrows as if surprised then rubbed his chin. "My number one suspect would be the Coalition Against Christmas. Only, I'm not sure anyone in the organization is capable of murder. They're certainly capable of trying to ruin Christmas, though."

I blinked, certain that I hadn't heard him correctly. "There's a Coalition Against Christmas?"

He did that throaty chuckle that always made me want to ask if he wanted a Scooby Snack. "Yeah, the organization is bigger than you would think. It's their goal to destroy anything that hints of religion, specifically at Christmastime."

"Don't people have anything better to do?"

He shrugged. "Apparently not. There is a war on religion, you know. We have to be tolerant of everyone and everything except Christians and Christian beliefs and traditions. It's the new American way."

"So I've heard." I crossed my arms, realizing with a touch of shame that I'd been on the other side once. I was just now starting to come around to another way of thinking and considering giving Jesus a chance. But I wasn't sure I really wanted to jump in on either side of this "war." "Tell me about this Coalition."

Pastor Shaggy's voice suddenly lost its laidback twang as passion tinged his words. "They're determined to get Christmas taken out of everything. They're not even that fond of the word 'holiday' anymore, but it's more acceptable than Christmas. They keep filing lawsuits against anyone or any organization that dares mention Christmas."

"Can they do that?"

"They can, and they do. They had one local school remove all songs about Christmas from their program. But what really bothered me was when a little girl drew a picture of the nativity scene and the art teacher hung it in the hallway. The school administration forced her to take it down."

"Have any names for this Coalition?"

"The local contact is Marvin Harris. I can do you even better." Pastor Shaggy reached into his pocket. "Here's the phone number and address of his local office."

***

The next thing I knew, I was driving down the street, ready to pay Marvin Harris a visit. I had no work lined up for the day, so why not? Maybe he would be surprisingly nice and point me in the right direction. Maybe his moral compass wasn't totally screwed up.

But, when I walked into his office at the M. H. Company and saw the immense scowl on his face, I figured I was wrong. Apparently, he owned a company that made cardboard boxes by day and was president of the local chapter of the Coalition Against Christmas by night. Owning a cardboard box company just might be reason enough to be utterly miserable. Quite possibly, the man also wore a near-real-looking Scrooge mask when he became his alter ego.

I'd told his secretary that I had to see him now. I may have even mentioned something about being from the coalition's corporate office.

One look at my jeans and long sleeved T-shirt, and Marvin Harris had to have known I wasn't.

"Mr. Harris, I'm Gabby St. Claire." I extended my hand. He didn't take it. Instead, he stared at me from his oversized desk, which was filled with mounds of papers and files. Around the perimeter of the room were boxes and on the walls were pictures of snakes, which I found to be rather creepy.

I halfway expected him to spit out, "Ba-humbug!" He didn't. Instead, he stared at me. Finally, he said, "What brings you here, Ms. St. Claire? Unannounced and under false pretenses, I might add."

I plopped myself into the chair across from him. "I'm wondering if you might help me to figure out who's trying to destroy Christmas."

He leaned closer. "I am."

It couldn't be that easy. I'd never, ever gotten a confession that quickly. "You? Really? Is it okay if I tell the police that?" I had to tread carefully. I had a knack for nearly getting myself killed.

He leaned back, his eyebrows shooting up. "The police? What do they have to do with this? Unless they're the pro-Christmas brigade."

Wow, he was not a sunny person, was he? "No, but someone has been vandalizing Christmas decorations around town, and I'm trying to figure out who." I purposely left out the information on the body parts, wanting to gage his reaction to some less morbid news first.

He leaned back, his lips pursed thoughtfully. "Vandalizing? Christmas decorations? Interesting. But I can't help. I know nothing about it. I'm certainly not responsible, but I'm certainly not displeased to hear this, either."

"You do realize that people have the right to worship as they please. They do have freedom of religion, and putting evidence of their faith and beliefs in their front yard isn't a crime."

He scowled again. "It should be. At the very least, it's a badge proclaiming to the world that they're idiots."

I straightened my back. Just who did this man think he was? "What gives you the right to think you're better than everyone else, Mr. Harris?"

"Religion is for the weak. It's a crutch. But it's not just the religious that I'm concerned about. It's anyone who wants to push their views down my throat." He scowled at me. "Like you."

"But aren't you trying to push your views down other people's throats?"

His face reddened into a dark, menacing scarlet. "Young lady, I think it's time you leave."

Why did people always say that? I stood. I really didn't think this man was guilty. I mean, he had some serious issues, but was he destroying nativity scenes? I doubted it. I didn't bother to offer him my hand this time.

But I did call over my shoulder, "Merry Christmas!" as I departed.

Man, it had never felt so good to say those words.

Chapter 4

Santa Claus Is Killing in Town

Marvin Harris had been my best lead. So where did that leave me now? I had two choices that had materialized in my mind. I could go home to a plain, lopsided Christmas tree that I wasn't sure would ever get decorated. Or I could go to The Grounds.

I was going to The Grounds—and for more than one reason. I could investigate and get a good cup of coffee in the process.

I strode up to Sharon, the pink-haired and more-piercings-than-a-pin-cushion owner of the place. "Any chance I could look at the video footage from your security cameras?"

I wondered if I looked at the video, if I'd pick up on something—anything—strange that had gone on outside of my apartment on yesterday evening. I was pretty sure that one of the cameras would include a glimpse of my parking lot.

She shrugged and pointed behind her to the cubbyhole she called an office. "Sure, have at it. I'm not sure how much you'll be able to see, though."

I decided it was worth a shot. I sat in a chair at her crowded desk and figured out how to review the tape. I'd done it a couple of times before, so it wasn't too hard. I found the time stamp for yesterday evening and hit play. I saw groups of college kids walking past, numerous cars, and a couple with their dog. What I didn't see was anyone get close to our apartment building.

Until I got to ten o'clock. That's when I saw a figure dressed in black creeping close to the building. I held my breath. What were they going to do? I mean, I knew what they were going to do, but how exactly were they going to do it?

The figure in front of my apartment building looked around. Then he grabbed the manger and put it in a sack, hoisted it onto his back and disappeared around the backside of the house. He returned a few minutes later and dumped out pieces of the scene into their original spot.

Interesting.

But who was it? I needed to get a better look at his face.

He walked back toward the street. It couldn't be this easy, could it?

Apparently it was. The man walked right up to the coffee shop. As he got closer, he looked up at the camera.

I moaned when I saw the man's face.

He was Santa Claus. Of course.

***

I rewound the tape and watched it over and over and over again, looking for something— anything—that might set this Santa apart from any other Santa in the area. I couldn't find anything, unless you wanted to count the machete he apparently carried in his bag of presents. The tape was too grainy, the sky too dark, and the man's beard too darn big and furry.

I wandered back into the café section of the coffee house and leaned across the counter toward Sharon. I didn't drink alcohol—my dad was an alcoholic, so I'd seen the effects of the stuff firsthand—but this coffee house was my hangout, and Sharon was like my bartender I supposed. She was the one person who'd always been there to listen. She also threw me a couple of shifts here and there when I was low on cash, which readily made her one of my favorite people.

"Did you find anything?" She smacked her gum as she wiped down the counters.

"Maybe. Did you see someone dressed like Santa come in last night?"

She glanced up, staring at me for a moment, before going back to her intense wiping. "No. Why?"

"The person who destroyed that manger scene was dressed like Santa."

"I hate to tell you this, but we have a lot of people dressed like Santa come in here. There's an annual meeting of Santas that takes place in here every Christmas."

"No . . . " I thought goofy meetings like that only took place in my twisted imagination.

"I'm serious, Gabby. It started around five years ago. About twelve of them meet in here once a year to tell crazy stories about the Christmas season. It's great fun to listen to them."

I'd bet it was. "When are they meeting this year?"

"Tonight." She stopped wiping long enough to grin.

It looks like I had plans for the evening after all.

***

That evening, Riley and I walked into The Grounds. I blinked at what I saw there. Sure enough, a dozen men—and one woman?—dressed like Santa all sat in the corner with glasses of milk. Okay, they were actually mugs of coffee and lattes. But didn't milk sound so much cozier? All they needed was a plate full of cookies and a sign reading "For Santa" written in four-year-old scrawl.

We sat at the nearest table, and I tried to look casual. Apparently, I'm not very good at looking casual because Riley reached across the table and rubbed my shoulders until I loosened up some. The Santas were talking about the weather, so I tuned them out for a moment and tried to unwind.

"Busy day?" Riley asked.

"Chad and I were at a crime scene, a non-fatal shooting." It hadn't taken us long to clean, and I made enough money to buy groceries for the week, which meant I could eat, which was always a plus.

The Santas began sharing children horror stories—the criers, the biters, the kickers. Riley and I smiled across the table at each other.

What would it be like if Riley and I had children one day? Would we take them to sit on Santa's lap? Would we even teach them about Santa? Riley was a devout Christian, and I wasn't sure if someone as devoted as he was would perpetrate a ruse on his own kids.

But, of course, I went there. Again. When would I ever learn to stop dreaming about a future with the man?

I tried to get a good look at the Santas, tried to see if there was anything that would allow me to identify the man from the video. I was highly doubtful, but I'd gone on lesser leads before.

Sometimes it was the leads you were sure *wouldn't* pan out that actually turned out to be the most valuable.

An hour later, I'd heard about which malls you didn't want to work at, which parties paid the best, and which charities were looking for volunteers. What I hadn't heard was anything that would help me.

That's when I decided to take matters into my own hands. I stood, cringing as my chair scraped across the floor. Riley had just started to mutter my name when I approached the group of jolly old St. Nicks.

"Have you guys heard about the Christmas scenes that have been destroyed in this area?"

The conversation went North Pole cold and everyone stared up at me. Finally, one brave soul— a twenty-something-year-old kid with the worst looking fake beard ever—spoke up. "I did hear about that."

"Anyone know of an angry Santa who might be behind it?"

"An angry Santa? You think one of us is guilty? For the love of stocking stuffers, you're off your rocker, lady," said a grandfatherly Santa with a real—but brittle—white beard.

There were many approaches I could have taken at this point. I decided to play naughty instead of nice. "Maybe. There's a rumor that the person is dressing up just like you."

I was pretty sure that was a collective gasp if I'd ever heard one.

"Anyone can get a Santa costume, lady. You're crazy if you think one of us is behind it." Brooklyn Santa spoke up from the other side of the table.

If I wasn't careful, I might have an angry mob of Santas throwing coal at me. Maybe I should tread more carefully. "I didn't say one of you were behind it. But I thought you might have some information."

Riley appeared beside me. "We're just looking for information. We're not accusing anyone." He gave me a lingering look that clearly reminded me of my promise to use all of my caution and logic.

"We all love Christmas," Brooklyn Santa said. "You're climbing into the wrong sleigh here, little lady."

I shoved a picture from my purse at him. "Does anyone recognize this man?"

The picture moved from hand to hand, each person shaking their heads and mumbling things like, "I have no idea," "don't recognize him," "beats me."

I needed more information and fast. The problem was, I didn't even know what to ask because the lead had proven to be pretty pointless. "Is there a place in this area that's known for renting Santa costumes? You have to admit that the beard looks pretty authentic."

"That's easy," Brooklyn Santa said. "Try Chadwick's on 21st Street. They've got the best suits there."

Chadwick's? Interesting. A Christmas-green light bulb flashed on in my head. The chicken wire nativity scene lady had mentioned that store also. And that couldn't be a coincidence.

***

The next morning, my cell phone rang at 8 a.m. It was Charity, the woman Pastor Shaggy had a thing for.

"You remember me from yesterday?"

"Of course." I pushed myself up in bed.

"Well, I was talking to the pastor yesterday, and he told me what you were doing. I don't know if this will help or not, but he encouraged me to let you know about a possible suspect."

Her words were like feather dusters to the cobwebs in my brain. I was suddenly alert. "Go on."

"As a teacher, I always have to take on part-time jobs to make ends meet. That said, I used to work for a local mall. Someone complained about our Merry Christmas signs last year and threatened to bring a lawsuit against us if we didn't remove them."

"Was it the Coalition Against Christmas?"

"No, actually, it wasn't. It was a man named Oliver Nichols. He's an atheist. Apparently, he's brought lawsuits against other businesses in the area. He has some kind of tragic back-story. I guess his father died on Christmas, and he's hated the holiday and God ever since then."

"That is tragic." Although part of me could relate. My brother had been kidnapped and my mother had died, leaving just me and a freeloading father who'd rather keep company with Jack Daniels more than anyone else. "Do you have any idea where I might find Mr. Nichols?"

"He actually wrote a book on why Christmas is of the devil. He's doing a book signing today in downtown Norfolk. I thought you should know."

"That's really helpful, Charity. Thanks for the information."

"No problem, Gabby. I hope you catch this guy."

"Will you let me know if anything like that happens at the mall again this year?"

"I would, but I took a different part-time job a few months ago. This one has better hours."

"Got it."

I didn't have any jobs lined up for the day, and since Chad decided to drive to the mountains and get some snowboarding in, that meant I could investigate the case as much as I wanted today without any guilt that I was neglecting my responsibilities.

The first place I would visit was the costume shop.

On my way out the door, I glanced over at my pitiful looking Christmas tree. I'd bought that one because it seemed neglected. But here in my apartment it still seemed neglected, and that was all my fault. I needed to do something about that later.

When I stepped out of my apartment, Riley was waiting there with two cups of to-go coffee in hand. He leaned against the wall, his hair still shiny wet as if he'd just stepped out the shower.

I stared at him a moment, feeling like he'd read my mind and knew I had "trouble" on my radar. "How'd you know?"

He stood and shrugged, a small smile playing across his lips as he thrust the coffee into my hands. "I've known you awhile now. I know how you think."

"How long have you been waiting out here for me?" I took a sip and savored the caffeinated warmth that filled me as we started down the steps.

"Only a few minutes. I wanted to catch you

before you left. I know you're investigating today and want to go with you, if that's okay."

"If you insist." Some company would be nice. Especially Riley's company.

"You're still coming to the Living Christmas Tree aren't you?"

We climbed into his car. "I wouldn't miss seeing you singing while standing in evergreen formation. Are you wearing tights also? Maybe an elf costume?"

He chuckled as we started down the road. "You have a way with words, Gabby. That's just one more thing I love about you. And, no, I'm not. We will be dressed in red and green, however."

"Well, maybe you can find an outfit at the costume shop. I really think the tights would be a good idea."

The shop was only a few minutes away. We parked and made our way inside the store. The woman behind the counter, oddly enough, reminded me of Mrs. Claus with her gray hair pulled back into a bun, the tiny wire-framed glasses she wore, and her hefty figure. She looked like the sweet grandmotherly type as she pored over some papers with a pen in hand. I knew Arlene said the woman was difficult, but I just couldn't picture it.

I plastered on a grin as I approached the counter and pulled out the picture. "I know it's not much to go on, but do you recognize anything about this picture? The costume? The person wearing it?"

She put the pen down and, with her glasses on the end of her nose, stared at the picture. "It's 'not much to go on' is right. I'm afraid I can't help you. Not that I would, even if I could. There is something called the 'right to privacy.' Ever heard of it?" She shook her head and handed the paper back to me.

So much for the sweet Mrs. Claus image I had. "Are you sure? It's very important."

Her beady eyes narrowed at me. "Quite certain. Did I stutter the first time?"

Wow. That was all I could say. Mentally, at least. "Do you have a record of who might have purchased a beard like that over the past couple of weeks?"

"Young lady, we don't keep that kind of inventory. It would take up too much time if we did. Do you have any idea of what's involved in running a small business?"

"I do, actually."

Someone else stepped into the shop. "Then you'll understand why paying customers are priority. Good day."

I couldn't resist calling over my shoulder as I left, "If you talk to your husband, tell him that all I want for Christmas is my two front teeth . . . or maybe a hippopotamus."

"Gabby . . . " Riley shook his head and chuckled. "You have a way with words. Have I ever told you that before?"

"Maybe once or twice." We walked out the door and onto the busy street where Christmas shoppers carried bags upon bags of what I presumed to be gifts. "Well, that was a waste of time. That woman could take joy in human form and body slam it senseless."

"Sometimes you have to turn over a lot of rocks before you find what you're looking for." He glanced over at me. "What next?"

"Next, we're going to a book signing."

"Why are we going to a book signing?"

"Come on and I'll show you."

***

The crowd of people waiting to see Oliver Nichols was larger than I'd anticipated. A big sign hung at the front of the store reading "The 12 Crimes of Christmas." Apparently, this man thought anything having to do with Christmas was a crime. Riley and I joined the crowds, no book in hand.

On second thought, maybe I should buy a book. If he was guilty, maybe there was a clue inside.

I grabbed a copy at the last minute and joined a bunch of sour-faced people who were waiting in line. As much as I wanted to talk to Riley, I decided I wanted to listen to the conversations around me even more.

My ears immediately perked when I heard mention of the crimes taking place around town. The conversation was between two middle-aged people in front of me—a tall man with graying hair and a plump woman with poofs of dyed red hair around her face. I couldn't help but wonder if that's what I would look like in twenty years? I didn't dwell on that thought long, though.

"Someone blowing up a nativity scene. Now that's a hoot," the woman said. "I wish I had thought of it."

"There are a few other things I'd like to blow up," the man muttered. "But I don't think violence is the answer. I just fantasize about it. It's about time we had an anti-Christmas vigilante. He's like Robin Hood for our types."

Did they know about the human hair or ear found at the scenes? I was pretty sure the police hadn't released that information. At least, I hadn't heard about it if they had.

We moved four steps closer.

"This book," the woman raised her copy. "This book should be reading for every elementary school child. It's well written and well thought out. As far as I'm concerned, this war on Christmas is just starting. Those religious folk think they own our country, that they're morally superior. It's time to let them know they're not."

"Preach it."

The man and woman laughed.

What a polarized society we've become, I thought.

Suddenly, I felt old fashioned. Was I out of touch with reality? Was this the way people were starting to think? Was I the one behind the times?

I didn't know the answers to those questions. At one point in my life, I'd felt so certain of so many things. It seemed with age, I experienced more doubts and saw more gray areas.

Riley might say that God was working on me, that he was trying to soften and change my heart. I just didn't know.

We crept a few steps closer again, and I got a better look at Oliver Nichols. He was probably in his forties with salt and pepper hair, a full mustache and artsy glasses. He smiled at customers, but the action never quite reached his eyes. He signed, handed the book to the customer, and motioned for the next customer to shuffle forward.

Most of the people in line ahead of me considered him a crusader. I wasn't sure what I considered him except unhappy, and that was simply based on my gut feeling.

Just as we approached, Riley leaned forward and whispered, "Easy." Just the feeling of his breath on my cheek was enough to send shivers scrambling down my spine.

All those shivers disappeared as I thrust my book at the man. "Sign, please."

His head remained down, but his eyes flickered up at me. "Anything you'd like me to say?"

I shrugged. "Feliz Navidad?"

His eyes narrowed and he stroked his name over the page and pushed it toward me. His gaze was already on the person behind me in line. He wasn't getting off the hook that easily.

"What do you think of everything happening around town?" I asked. I shifted so the man behind me couldn't step forward. Finally, Oliver raised his head. I offered a wide grin.

He scowled. "I think someone's trying to send a message."

I leaned closer and lowered my voice. "It's secretly you, isn't it? It would be great publicity for your new book."

His scowl deepened. "I prefer the word to the sword, ma'am."

"If you hear who's doing it, would you give me a call?" I slipped my business card toward him.

He stared at it a moment. "Gabby St. Claire? Crime scene cleaner? I'm not sure I understand the association."

"What's happening to Christmas is a crime," I explained.

He stared—again. Finally, he reached into his pocket and handed me something. "Call me and we'll talk."

I raised my eyebrows and took his card. Then I flashed my most winning smile his way and thanked him.

He'd seemed helpful. Too helpful? I wasn't sure.

But I planned on finding out.

Just before I slipped outside, a woman at the back of the line caught my eye. The owner of Chadwick's on 21st—Mrs. Santa Claus's sour twin sister.

I stored that information in the back of my mind. Maybe it would be useful later.

Chapter 5

It Came Upon a Midnight Crime

As soon as I got to the parking lot, I paused and dialed Oliver Nichols's number. I couldn't believe it when he answered on the third ring. "Oliver?"

"Yes?" I could hear the crowds of people around him still.

"This is Gabby St. Claire. You said to call you."

"I just gave you my card ten minutes ago, Ms. St. Claire. I'm still doing my book signing."

I glanced through the massive windows at the front of the store and saw that he'd spotted me. I offered a friendly wave. "You answer your phone during book signings? I'm pretty sure there's some rule against that."

"Listen, Ms. St. Claire, I'll call you later. I would like to talk."

"Perfect. Thank you." I hung up and glanced at Riley, who leaned against his car with his arms crossed and a grin across his too-handsome-for-my-comfort face.

Riley shook his head at me, his eyes

twinkling with amusement. "You did not just do that."

"I did. We don't really have any time to waste. There have been human remains left at crime scenes. I think that makes this matter more urgent."

"Except nothing was left when they destroyed the manger outside our apartment. I wonder why."

I shrugged. "Maybe destroying that was an afterthought."

"You mean, maybe someone discovered you were at both of the previous two crime scenes and decided to send a message?"

"Or maybe they discovered that *you* were at both crime scenes."

He sighed. "I just have a bad feeling about this." He stood and stared at me a moment before finally asking, "Do you want to talk about this more over lunch?"

I was hungry now that he mentioned it. And cold. I really wanted to get out of this wind. "Sure thing."

A few minutes later, we pulled up to The Happy Flounder, a restaurant overlooking the Elizabeth River in downtown Norfolk. We were seated in a booth at the upscale version of Long John Silvers. Riley ordered shrimp scampi, and I got a crab cake and fries. Neither of us would win the healthy eating award for the day. Before Riley could steer the subject into a safe topic, I opened Oliver Nichols's book and scanned the chapter headings. Riley leaned in closer to look at the book. I caught a whiff of his spicy aftershave and flutters tickled my spine.

I shoved those feelings aside and stared at the pages. "He actually doesn't seem as angry as Marvin did. He seems more like an intellectual."

Riley's elbows rested on the table, and he tilted his head in a casual manner that seemed awfully lawyer-ish. "So, you agree with his writings then?"

I closed the book and leaned back into the hard vinyl behind me. My gaze scanned the river behind Riley. Picture windows opened up the entire wall and the view was breathtaking. Of course, I always had a good view when Riley sat across from me.

Riley stared at me a moment, and my face flushed. I didn't say that aloud did I? *Please say I didn't say that aloud.*

Riley said nothing, so I assumed I'd kept my thoughts to myself and settled back into the matters at hand. "In order to have the separation of church and state, I don't believe that we have to pretend like our country wasn't founded on

Christian principles. Christian or not, the Ten
Commandments are a good moral foundation for
anyone."

He raised his eyebrows and nodded
thoughtfully. The waitress brought us both some
water, and Riley shoved a black straw into his glass.
"Well said." He leaned closer, close enough that my
traitorous heart sped. "Is it so hard for you to
believe that the Son of God was born here on
earth?"

"It's such a dainty little notion, Riley. But, I
really don't know. I can probably accept that Jesus
came to earth, but I just can't picture the creator of
the entire universe dying for a bunch of people who
either don't believe in him or who outright hate
him." I frowned, wondering if my answer
disappointed him. I took a turn at stabbing the
lemon in my water glass with my straw before
shrugging. "That's the truth."

"I don't want you to lie to me."

"I just wish that faith came easily to me."

"Faith is a choice I make every day, Gabby."

"Really?" It just seemed like faith and
believing and being good just came so easily to
Riley.

"Really. Every believer has doubts
sometimes. That's what makes faith, faith—when
you can overcome those doubts and still believe."

He did his head tilt again. "Did you ever believe in Santa Claus?"

I shook my head and ran my finger along the condensation on my glass. "Never."

"Really?"

I nodded slowly. "Really." We were saying that word a lot, weren't we? "We didn't have a chimney, for starters. I knew one man couldn't deliver presents to millions of children in the course of mere hours. Even from a young age, I didn't buy it."

Riley leaned back and laughed. "I should have known your parents couldn't get one past you. Even in elementary school, you had a knack for investigating. I love that."

"How about you? Did your parents teach you about Santa?" I didn't really know a lot about his parents. I imagined them to be uppity and morally superior, but then again, they'd raised such a great guy in Riley, maybe they weren't.

"As a matter of fact . . . no, they didn't." He took a sip of his water.

I put my hand over my heart in mock drama. "They were that cruel? At least my parents tried."

His smile told me that I hadn't offended him. Thank goodness. "My parents thought they'd be lying to me if they told me a man in a red suit delivered my presents."

"Do you wish they had? Do you wish you'd felt that magic of Christmas?"

"Not really. I mean, sure, it sounds like fun. But I respect them for keeping it real. They made sure that Christmas wasn't all about gifts and getting and materialism."

"How'd they do that?"

"We always delivered gifts to less fortunate families—nursing home residents, homeless shelters, foster care children. They also encouraged us to use our own money to buy gifts for others. And they were never extravagant. They didn't indulge us or run up their credit card bills or wallow in commercialism. Christmas was about celebrating Jesus."

The idea sounded nice, but what did it look like in reality? "And just how do you do that? By singing songs? By going to church?"

"Those things are good and worthy. But I think the best way to celebrate is by giving to others, by reflecting Christ's love in that way."

"Are you doing those things with your family this year?"

He shrugged. "I'm not sure if I'm going to make it home or not. Besides, my parents may be headed up north to spend Christmas with my brother and his family."

"You strike me as the type who wouldn't

miss Christmas with your family. You'd go over the river and through the woods."

"Normally I would try to. But sometimes you have to make the best decision for yourself. I'm just getting this practice off the ground, and I'm not sure I can afford the time away. Plus, I promised to drop by the Brambleton Homeless Shelter and help serve food."

The waitress set our steaming plates before us. Riley looked up at me as I grabbed my silverware. "Is it okay if I pray for us?"

"Of course."

I closed my eyes and listened to his prayer. It sounded sincere, like he was talking to a real person and not just some imaginary friend. What would it be like to have a faith that real? To believe so firmly in something you couldn't see or feel or touch? He said "amen," and I opened my eyes.

Riley began twirling some pasta around his fork. "So what are your thoughts on everything so far?"

I picked up a fry. "Well, I think the Redskins are horrible this year, the weatherman is always wrong, that politics are annoying—"

He paused with his fork mid-bite. "On everything with the case, Gabby. Everything with the case."

"Oh," I said in mock realization. I jabbed my

fry into the ketchup. "I don't know. It's kind of creepy, isn't it? I keep trying to nail the M.O. of the person who would do this. It was one thing when they only destroyed some decorations. I mean, that wasn't nice and all, but human remains? That's weird. Someone's trying to send a deeper message than I ever anticipated."

"Vandalism is one thing, but this has turned into a murder investigation. Who would have that kind of fury?"

"Maybe we're looking in the wrong direction. Maybe this isn't about Christmas at all. Maybe this is about murder and they're using symbols of Christmas to distract us."

"Could be. Who's on your radar so far?"

"There's a man who heads up the Coalition Against Christmas and there's Oliver Nichols. Beyond those two men, I don't have any other suspects."

"Those are two pretty good suspects, I'd say."

I shrugged. "There's less than a week until Christmas. So far, three crimes—that we know about—have been committed. First, it was the chicken wire nativity scene, then the church manger scene, and finally that manger in front of our apartment. What's going to happen next?"

My cell phone rang. I glanced at my screen and then back up at Riley. "It's Oliver Nichols."

"You must have powers of persuasion."

But did I? This almost seemed too easy. I put the phone to my ear and answered.

"Let's meet."

"I'm at The Happy Flounder. Wanna swing by?"

"Give me ten minutes."

***

Twenty minutes later, Oliver Nichols showed up, just as "Holly, Jolly Christmas" began playing on the overhead. I wondered if he was going to bypass talking to us so he could complain to the manager.

Instead, he came right over to us, an almost angry energy in his quick, heavy steps. He'd donned a long black trench coat and had tucked a blue silky scarf around his neck that gave him a crazy rich person vibe.

He stood at the end of the table, staring at Riley on one side of the booth and me on the other. Finally, he grabbed a chair from an empty table, pulled it up between us, and straddled it. He folded his arms across the back as if he were modeling for a photo shoot.

"I'm not behind this," he started.

I pushed away my empty plate. "I didn't say you were." Not directly, at least. Or did I? "Why did you want to meet with us?"

His gaze shifted over to me. "Because the police questioned me earlier. I need to prove that I'm innocent."

I turned my palm up as I asked the question, "Why would they think you're guilty?"

He glanced from side to side before his shoulders drooped from the exhaustion of carrying too much . . . guilt? "I like sending out letters."

"Okay . . . " Where was this going?

He sighed and made eye contact with me again. His shoulders drooped even farther. "I might have sent one to that church whose nativity scene was blown to shreds."

Riley leaned forward, suddenly interested in the conversation. "What did this letter say exactly?"

Oliver's face reddened. The waitress approached but he shooed her away and turned back to us. "I might have called them idiots. But that doesn't mean I'm guilty."

And the plot thickens . . . I didn't say that aloud. At least, I didn't think I did.

I laced my fingers together in front of me, trying to look professional and intimidating. "From what I've heard, Mr. Nichols, you've sent lots of nasty-grams out to people in this area."

"I have, and I stand behind my letters. But I'm not a violent person." He slapped the table so hard that our glasses jumped.

Riley shook his head, ever the unflustered one. "Why do you hate Christmas so much, Mr. Nichols? You've made it your life's work to get any mention of Christ taken out of anything public. Why?"

"I don't like having religion pushed down my throat."

The same thing Marvin Harris had told me. Apparently a lot of atheists felt this way. I was going to tell him what I'd told Marvin. "Other people don't like having your views pushed down their throats. Have you ever considered that?"

"We have freedom of speech and religion in this country. I don't want my tax dollars paying for something that promotes a certain viewpoint. It's unethical." Oliver's eyes narrowed and his nostrils flared. "Maybe you should talk to Marvin Harris with the Coalition Against Christmas."

"As a matter of fact, I did talk to him." Score one for Gabby.

"He's a hothead. I'd put my efforts into investigating him." He shook his head and raised a finger in the air, his voice becoming louder. "I do know this. I didn't kill anyone."

I don't usually mind making scenes, but even I had to pause and glance around the restaurant to count just how many people were staring at us now. By my estimates that would be all of the twenty-three or so people in line of sight.

"So the police talked to you, you said?"

He lowered his voice. "Yes, they talked to me. I wouldn't be here if it was just vandalism. Murder is another thing entirely. I'm a respected member of this community, and I plan to remain just that, Christmas or not."

"Are you planning any more demonstrations this year?"

He scowled. "I'm not sure."

"Might not be the best idea, huh?"

Or had he already done some demonstrations that he just hadn't owned up to yet?

***

Just as I climbed into Riley's car, anxious to rehash the conversation that had just taken place, my cell phone beeped again. I recognized the number as Chad's. If he was taking time away from skiing, then it had to be serious.

"What's up? Aren't you supposed to be dashing through the snow or something?" I closed the door quickly, hoping to ward away the bitter breeze that swept around us as it came over the waters of the Elizabeth River.

"Gabby, something's been bothering me about that hair found at the crime scene."

"Okay. What is it?" I pulled the seatbelt over my lap just as Riley cranked the engine and still-cold air began screaming through the vents.

"I think it belongs to a dead person."

"I would agree." Did he really have to call to tell me that? I shrugged at Riley, who stared at me with a "what's going on?" expression as he blew on his fingers to keep them warm.

"No, no, hear me out. I think it belongs to someone who's been dead, who's been embalmed for that matter."

Now he had my attention. "Why would you think that, Chad?"

"A couple of reasons. When someone's been embalmed, their skin turns pinkish. It also retains the scent of formalin, the flushing fluid used in the embalming process. If the scalp was from someone who'd just died, there would still be blood. The more I think about it, the more I realize that I'm right."

"Brilliant deductive reasoning, Sherlock. Maybe I should call Detective Adams." I felt myself lighting up like a Christmas tree. I had to admit that I was truly impressed. I motioned for Riley to start driving back toward our apartments. He backed out, and we began cruising down the road.

"My guess is that he already knows. He just might not be sharing that information with you."

I hated to admit that he was right. "I won't know unless I talk to him. And, in case I didn't tell you, you're brilliant. At least, you are when you're not playing with your toes."

I filled Riley in before calling the detective.

Detective Adams answered on the first ring. "It's your favorite Nosy Nelly."

"Hi, Gabby."

I smiled, stealing a glance at the outdoor ice skating rink outside of MacArthur Center Mall. I wish I felt as carefree as the smiling family sliding over the ice with their arms wrapped around each other. At least I had my case to investigate. My nosiness kept my mind occupied, if nothing else. "Detective, I have a theory that I wanted to pass along to you."

"Go ahead."

"I think the hair you found at the crime scene was from someone who'd been embalmed already."

"How'd you know that?"

"My colleague used to be a mortician."

Detective Adams grunted. "That's right. Good work."

"I guess you can't tell me anything else about it?" I held my hand up before the vent, where warm air was blowing out.

"Not at this time. But I do want to remind you to back off, Gabby. We don't know who we're dealing with here. You get that degree, Gabby, and then I'll put in a good word for you. You can investigate all you want after that with no complaints from me."

"Thank you." Warmth filled me. Maybe there was hope in sight. Just maybe.

But until then, we had a twisted killer—kind of—on our hands.

Chapter 6

Deck the Halls with Boughs of Folly

The next morning, Pastor Shaggy called and asked if Riley and I could visit someone from his congregation who'd called him in a panic. Something had happened at their house during the night, and they were hesitant to call the police. The incident apparently had something to do with the whole "war on Christmas" thing.

Just as we pulled into the neighborhood, I thought I saw a familiar face driving away in a yellow Volkswagen Beetle. Was that Charity? What was she doing in the neighborhood?

"What is it?" Riley asked as I craned my neck for a better look behind us.

I looked back at him, pointing with my thumb over my shoulder. "That looked like Charity."

"What would Charity be doing here?"

I shrugged. "I don't know. But didn't that look like her?"

"To be honest, I wasn't paying attention."

Riley pulled up to the house. I blanched as I

looked at the residence. A cheap plastic nativity scene had been placed—no, I should say strapped—to the roof of the house. Mary was on one side of the chimney, Joseph on the other, and baby Jesus was front and center. It looked like the holy family had been taken hostage.

Riley and I glanced at each other before climbing out of the car and knocking at the door. An overweight man in a bathrobe answered mid-knock, introduced himself as Warren, and ushered us inside. A petite, elderly woman with hair that still looked freshly permed—his mother, he said—sat on the well-worn, navy blue couch making angels out of tissue paper.

Riley and I sat on the other side of the couch. Riley leaned with his elbows on his knees toward the woman and in his best attorney's voice said, "Why don't you tell us what happened?"

"Yes, please explain how the Joseph, Mary and Jesus were taken hostage."

Warren grunted. "Taken hostage? What are you talking about?"

I pointed above me. "Someone tied them to the roof."

He glared. "That's where I put them. On the roof where everyone could see them. I had to tie them there so they wouldn't fall off."

I cleared my throat. "Sorry. Continue, please."

"We were sleeping," the woman started, wiping her eye with the back of her hand. Her voice sounded as frail and thin as she looked. "Then we heard something up on the housetop."

I closed my eyes, feeling sure this was a practical joke. It had all the right elements. Still, I kept my mouth shut. "Go on."

She glanced at us, her eyes red-rimmed and dispelling my fear of being punked. "I'd read in the newspaper about some of the crimes being committed around town, so I worried someone was trying to sabotage our Christmas scene on the roof."

Warren turned toward us. "As you can see, nothing happened to the scene. But something was dropped down our chimney."

"It wasn't a big fat man in a red suit, was it?" The words slipped out before I could stop them.

Riley elbowed me, and I clamped my lips together.

The woman reached out and lifted a wooden box from the coffee table. "No, it was this."

She handed it to me. I slowly opened the box and saw the note reading "Gold, Frankincense, and Myrrh." Inside, there were two vials of some kind of liquid I couldn't identify. A ring box held . . . a gold tooth. I turned to Riley. "How much do you want to bet this is from the same person the hair and the ear was taken from?"

Another paper rested beneath all of it.

The words scrawled there read, "Deck the Halls with Boughs of Folly."

Folly. That seemed like a good description for what was going on. I stood and shook my head. "Are you sure you don't want to call the police?"

The man shook his head. "Before I was a Christian, I was into some pretty bad things."

"What kind of things?" This could be important to the case, I told myself. Or I could just be nosy.

He scowled. "Things like drugs. I did some time. Did some probation. But now I'm clean, and I don't like to call attention to myself from the police, ever. Never. If I mess up one more time, they'll throw me in jail for good. This has to stay between us."

I tried to keep him logical. "But Warren, this could be major evidence. It could help put the bad guy behind bars."

"No police!" The man sliced his hand through the air. "If you call them, I'll deny everything."

I nodded and held up the vials again. Just what was inside? "Okay, how about this? Can I take these with me? I won't tell anyone where I got them."

"You're not going to sell me out?"

I shook my head. "No, I won't."

Warren stared at me another moment before nodding. "Fine, then."

Great, so now I had some evidence. But what would I do with it in order to not implicate Warren or to get myself arrested?

***

Apparently, we had just enough time to make it to church after we visited the family. Despite insisting I was inappropriately dressed for church in my jeans and red sweater—the red sweater not in honor of Christmas, but because I liked red— Riley insisted harder we were fine as we parked outside of a high school gym.

Yes, his church met at a school. I'd pegged Riley as the uptight type before I really got to know him. I thought he'd be all about wearing just the right clothes and acting perfect, but he wasn't. That had become amazingly clear when his long-forgotten fiancée showed up at my doorstep, just as I'd thought our relationship was taking off.

Go me.

But that was all water under the Christmas tree now.

"Wait!" I yanked on his arm before he exited his car.

"What?"

I pulled the vial out of my pocket and began to twist the top off. "You know I can't wait. I couldn't open it while you were driving. I was afraid I might spill it."

His hand came over mine. "You don't know what's inside. Be careful."

"Of course." I slipped the top off and slowly brought the vial up under my nose. I braced myself for what I might smell. As soon as the scent hit me, I recognized it. "Formaldehyde."

Riley blinked. "You mean the chemical that's used on the frogs we used to dissect in high school?"

"Or in embalming."

We exchanged a glance before I unscrewed the other vial. I couldn't smell anything. "As far as I'm concerned, it has no scent, almost like water."

"What could it be? Besides water?"

I shrugged. "I have no idea." I squeezed my lips together as I put the top back on. "I can't keep this from Detective Adams."

Riley shook his head. "No, you can't. You don't want to be charged with obstruction of justice. That tooth could belong to the same person whose hair and ear was found, too. Maybe it's from the same person . . . but maybe it's not. Either way, you have to hand it over to the authorities."

"You're right." My heart felt heavy as I said

the words. I wanted to keep my promise, but I also wanted to keep everything legal. I really needed to think on what to do.

Inside, about one hundred and fifty people filled the auditorium as a band played Christmas carols on the stage—a more updated version of them, at least. After they finished, everyone sat down and Pastor Shaggy came on stage. He preached about the war on Christmas and how our battle was not against flesh and blood, which, of course, made me think of that bloody scalp.

If only I had access to the same information as the police did...that's why I had to get my degree. Then I could effectively work cases like this and track down the bad guys. I would, in my own way, be able to leave my mark on the world.

After church was over, Riley and I lingered in the back. Charity marched toward us, a bright smile on her face. "Good to see you here, Gabby. How's the case coming?"

I shrugged. "We're tracking down some new leads."

"Did Oliver Nichols turn up anything interesting?"

"No, Oliver Nichols didn't really give us much information. He seems to think that Marvin Harris might be the guilty one."

Charity's eyes widened and she opened her

mouth to speak, but no words came out. I looked over and saw Pastor Shaggy approaching. The woman was in love. How cute. I really hoped that I didn't look like that when Riley approached me, however.

I still wanted to ask her if she drove a Yellow Beetle, but I'd wait until later, when Pastor Shaggy was out of earshot.

Pastor Shaggy reached us and extended his hand, a lopsided grin across his face. "Gabby St. Claire. It's a pleasure, as always."

I leaned toward him. "What happened on your forehead?"

He touched the scrape there. It hadn't been visible when he was on stage because his hair covered it. But, now that he was closer, I cringed at the cut that stretched across the top of his head. I remembered forgetting to ask about the scrape on his hand at that meeting a couple of days ago. What was going on?

"One of the stairs leading to my apartment gave out this morning. I crashed all the way down to the bottom of the landing, hitting my head on the way."

I cringed. "Ouch."

"Yeah, it was weird. Those steps are new. The landlord had them replaced about a month ago. I have no idea why one would split down the middle."

He didn't, but that was because his thoughts were all pure and holy. Mine weren't. My hands went to my hips. "I want to see these stairs."

Riley's eyes met mine. "Why? You're not thinking . . . "

"Someone's trying to destroy Christmas. What better person to target than the person behind the effort to save it?"

***

I stood, brushing some winter-crisp leaves from my jeans, and shook my head. I grabbed ahold of the stair railing to keep my balance and looked down at the three others who were with me.

"Someone definitely tampered with that step, Pastor. You need to watch out. I don't know what they might be planning next."

"Why are you so certain?" Riley asked.

I pointed to the area where the step was broken. "Look at the way the wood is split. The lines are pretty clean. If this had happened because the wood was simply weak, then there would be more splintering."

"Maybe the contractor who put the step in didn't know what he was doing and used a damaged piece of wood," Charity offered.

Pastor Shaggy shook his head. He pushed past Charity and got a closer look before standing and frowning. "That might explain the glass in my mailbox."

"The glass in your mailbox?" I hadn't heard about that yet.

He reached for the cut across his thumb. "I reached in to get something the other day and found that someone had left a broken bottle in there. I didn't even see it. It got me good. I guess I really am in danger."

I'd seen that cut last Friday and planned to ask him what happened. I'd gotten distracted by everything else, though. "You should be careful until this person is caught. All of this seems to be escalating, and now you're in the crosshairs."

We lumbered back down the stairs and stood on the crisp grass in front of his boxy, 70s era apartment building.

Charity looked up at Pastor Shaggy with her big brown eyes. "Maybe you should give it up. I don't want you to get hurt. Is it really worth it?"

I was pretty sure the pastor blushed. "I can't give up. If I do, I'll let the bully behind all of this win. Besides, God took care of Paul in prison and Daniel in the den of lions. I know he can take care of me, too."

I wanted to argue with him, but I couldn't. I

wasn't one for backing down, so I couldn't encourage the pastor to do it either. But I didn't want to see him get hurt.

That made the urgency of the situation even greater. Someone was now trying to hurt people. Real, living people. The glass and the broken stair might only be the beginning. What would they try next?

"Pastor! I'm glad I caught you!" A man came running out from an apartment on the first floor. "Someone stopped by yesterday to see you. He asked me to give you his card."

Pastor Shaggy took the card and stared at it a moment. "Marvin Harris."

"The Coalition Against Christmas!" My voice was louder than I intended. But then I found myself deflating as I put the facts together in my mind. "I'd say he was the one who messed with your step, but then why would he leave his contact information and implicate himself?"

Pastor Shaggy's neighbor shrugged. "He wasn't the most pleasant man. Rather abrupt and never smiled. I told him I'd pass this along, though."

The pastor thanked his neighbor and then we wandered down the street to a Mexican restaurant. The church crowd had already come and gone, so we were seated right away. Spanish Christmas carols, "Joy to the World" to be specific, played on the overhead as we slid into a booth. Riley and I sat on one side, and Pastor Shaggy and Charity on the other.

Is this what it would feel like to go on a double date? I mentally slammed on brakes. No, I couldn't go there. Instead of thinking of my own love life, I would focus on Pastor Shaggy, who looked awfully cozy with Charity.

Good. I was happy for him. He was a nice man, and he deserved to find someone.

I ordered some chicken enchiladas before munching on the crunchy chips and spicy salsa. Charity's gaze fell on me, and I paused mid-bite.

"So we didn't finish our earlier conversation. Anything you can share?" she asked.

I wiped my mouth and swallowed. "So far, we don't have any solid leads. One thing is clear, though. This person is trying to send a clear message that they don't like Christmas. I don't think they're trying to hurt anyone." I glanced at Pastor Shaggy. "Not seriously hurt them, at least. I think they're just trying to scare us away."

"What would give someone reason to hate Christmas that much?" Pastor Shaggy asked.

I shrugged. "My guess is they're either mentally unstable, they had a sad childhood, or both. But I'm no expert."

Charity took another sip of soda and shook

her head. "A sad childhood, huh? I guess I could relate to that one. My dad actually died on Christmas. He was in a car accident."

My heart pounded in my ears. "I'm sorry to hear that. My brother was kidnapped and my mom died a few years back, so I know how hard the holidays can be."

She sniffled. "It was awful for the first few years. Every Christmas I would just be reminded of all my losses. I would get depressed. I'd want to snap at anyone who actually looked joyful."

I understood.

Charity continued. "I knew that I could spend the rest of my life being resentful and hating Christmas for it, or I could use Christmas as just one more way to celebrate his life."

Pastor Shaggy craned his neck toward her. "And you choose to celebrate. That's just beautiful."

She smiled shyly. "Thanks. It's just one more reason I feel so passionate about this project that you've started."

"I couldn't have done all of this without you," Pastor Shaggy said.

I really felt like I should disappear and let the two of them have some time together. But that was impossible to do, especially with Riley here. Besides, I really needed a moment alone with Charity so I could ask her about this morning. I saw my opportunity when she stood to go to the restroom.

"Mind if I join you?" I asked, feeling way too girly for my own good. I was not a "herd mentality" kind of girl.

"Sure thing."

As we stood at the sink, I looked over at her. "Charity, were you over on Vaughn Street this morning?"

Her face went pale. "Vaughn Street? Why would you ask that?"

"Just answer. No games."

She sighed and then nodded. "I was. I was afraid you'd seen me."

"What were you doing there?"

"I've been feeling a little obsessed with this whole Christmas thing lately. The pastor told me what happened, and I just wanted to investigate myself. I know it's terrible, isn't it?"

I had no room to talk. I shook my head. "No, it's not terrible."

"Thanks for chatting, Gabby. I'm glad you felt comfortable enough to ask me instead of jumping to conclusions."

Right, because I never jumped to conclusions.

We slipped back to the table. At least one question had been cleared up. Just as my food arrived, my cell phone beeped. It was Chad. "So, I called a friend of mine who's a mortician in the area," he started.

"Why? You think a mortician is behind this?"

"Hear me out."

"Of course."

"I asked him if there were any morticians around here who could be behind this, who acted strangely, you know? Sometimes you just get that sense about people."

"Right."

"He said there was this one guy who always makes strange comments. My friend said he's always thought this guy could be guilty of lifting jewelry from dead people or something, you know? Maybe he's not doing that. Maybe he's doing something worse. Maybe he's leaving their body parts at crime scenes."

"You want to pay him a visit?"

"Tomorrow morning?"

"You've got it."

***

The next morning, Riley had a court date with one of his clients, so Chad and I headed out by ourselves. We pulled into an older community in the neighboring city of Chesapeake, stopping at the nicest house on the block. Weren't the nicest houses always the funeral homes? This one had been grand at one time with three levels and a turret to boot.

We strode up to the front door, which was unlocked, and walked inside. The lobby was empty and a little run down with matted gold carpet, shiny mahogany tables and extravagant flower arrangements in shades of mauve and country blue. Worse than that was the smell—musty and old. Not exactly what you want to smell when you pay honor to the deceased.

A thin woman with a neat but oversized black dress suit stepped from one of the side rooms. Her salt and pepper hair was pulled back into a tight bun and her dark eyes struck me as being ever perceptive. "Can I help you?"

"I was hoping to speak with Benjamin Videl," Chad started. "I'm a fellow mortician."

Her lips pulled into a tight line as she stared at us a moment. "I'm afraid he's busy right now."

"It's actually concerning an official investigation," I piped in. It was a good thing I'd decided to wear my one and only suit today. Perhaps I actually looked "official."

She blinked. "Investigation?"

I nodded. "We need his help. We've heard he's one of the best." As I always liked to say, flattery would get you everywhere.

Finally, she nodded. "One moment." She disappeared down a staircase.

I stared at the little breath mints on the table, along with the boxes of tissues. Wherever I looked, there seemed to be something to remind people of the name of the funeral home, complete with gold script and a curvy line at the bottom. Why did that logo look so familiar to me? Did they have some kind of advertising campaign on TV or somewhere?

Funeral homes were not my favorite place. Memories of my mom's memorial service flooded back to me. I remembered all the hugs from well-wishers, the sympathetic pats on the back, the total absence of emotion from my dad, who'd totally withdrawn in the days after her death. To be honest, he'd withdrawn before her death also; afterward it only got worse, though.

A moment later, a skeleton of a man crept up the stairs. He looked exactly as I thought a mortician might, complete with pale skin and black hair that had been slicked back from his face. He was tall, had a pointy nose, and overbearing eyebrows that just begged to be plucked.

This was our guy.

No, I couldn't think like that. Just because the man looked creepy as he came up from the dark basement of a creepy house didn't mean he was guilty.

"Can I help you?"

I was the first to extend my hand. Moist fingers met mine, and I wanted to cringe. "I'm Gabby St. Claire and we're looking into several suspicious incidents that have happened in the area lately. Someone told us you might be able to help."

Chad nudged himself in front of me. "And I'm Chad Davis. I'm a mortician by trade, but I gave that career up a while ago. It was starting to get to me."

The man's beady gaze slunk back and forth between both of us. His eyebrows were thick and heavy, adding to his brooding look. "How can I help?"

Chad and I glanced at each other before I finally jumped in. "It's like this. Someone's destroying Christmas displays in the area. Embalmed body parts have been found at the scene."

His eyebrows shot up. "You think I'm responsible?" His voice sounded eerily calm and steady, and he seemed deathly still.

Chad shook his head, shoving his hands down into his pockets. "We're wondering if you know who might be."

He shrugged, his eyes focused on Chad with somewhat of a cold calculation. "Why would I know?"

"We're chasing every lead, trying to figure

out if there are any morticians who are doing some shady things on the side."

"I know a few of my colleagues in the area." He dropped his head toward his shoulder. "But I'm not going to point the finger at any of them. It wouldn't be very professional." He crossed his arms over his bony chest and paused. "Why would someone do that?"

I shrugged this time. "Maybe they're not capable of murder, but they want to send a clear message."

"Well, I'm sorry, but I can't be of any help. I don't know any respectable person in this business who would do such a thing. It's horrendous and a disgrace to the profession." He glared at Chad. "You would understand that."

Chad's hands went to his hips in that casual way that he was known for. "You're right. I do realize that. But how else would someone be getting embalmed body parts?"

"Have you considered they might be grave diggers?" Benjamin stared at us, his eyes icy cold.

Grave diggers? I supposed that could be a possibility. But I had limited resources. There was no way I could check out every cemetery in this area for signs of vandalism. There was also no chance that Detective Adams would share that information with me.

Besides, there was something about this man that I found unsettling.

I glanced beyond him. The woman who'd greeted us stood in the dark, halfway down the staircase. She'd been listening the whole time but hadn't shown her face.

Was something strange going on here? Or was my imagination out of control simply because I was in a spooky old funeral home?

Chapter 7

Do You See What I See?

"Why aren't we moving?" Chad stared at me from the passenger seat.

I leaned back into my seat, turning down the radio, which had begun blaring "All I Want for Christmas Is You." It made my mind go places I didn't want it to go—places that included Riley and me having a happy-ever-after. That was one place that should never be visited because it was known as Delusionville.

I nodded toward the funeral home. "I want to follow him."

"Why? Because he looked like an oddball?"

"Maybe. I don't know. Something just seemed strange about our interaction. Don't you think?"

"Morticians work by themselves. That one works in the basement by himself. And he keeps company primarily with dead bodies. Sure, maybe there was something strange about him, but that doesn't mean he's behind these crimes."

"That doesn't mean he's not either." I

shrugged. "Besides, I don't have any more leads. I don't know where else to look and I have no desire to stake out a cemetery trying to figure out if someone is stealing dead bodies."

Chad grinned at me. "To see if Santa is stealing dead bodies, to be precise. You did say that's how the perpetrator was dressing."

"Yeah, how weird and Halloween-like would that be? The only thing that would make it weirder would be if they were leaving Thanksgiving meals behind as well."

"And Valentines. And maybe some Easter Eggs. Or fireworks."

"Aren't you funny?"

He rubbed the tips of his fingers on his shirt in mock cockiness. "I'd like to think so."

My lip curled in a half smile. "Just one more thing to love about you." As soon as I said the words, my smile slipped. I did not want him to get the wrong idea about love and me.

Thankfully, just at that moment, Benjamin Videl stepped out of the back door of the funeral home. He looked both directions before scurrying to a black sedan parked in the driveway. Chad and I were in my van, which was located in the parking lot of a church across the street. Thanks to my tinted windows, I didn't think he'd noticed me.

I eased out behind him, careful to stay a

respectable distance away.

Chad's feet remained propped up on the dashboard. He was as laidback as ever, which really did help to balance my neurotic impulsiveness. "What do you think this is going to prove, Gabby?"

"Nothing. Something. I don't know. Who do you think I am? Super Sleuth, Avenger of the Ghost of Christmas Present?"

"That has a nice ring to it. I kind of like it."

I slapped his arm. "Are you ever serious?"

"When we almost died back in November I was pretty serious."

I shuddered at the thought. Yes, he was. We both were. That happened when your life was on the line. And it all had been because of a fake Elvis. My life was anything but boring. I'd give it that.

He wound through the neighborhood and into Norfolk. As Benjamin pulled into a subdivision, he slowed in front of a house.

A house with thousands of lights and wooden figures, plastic figures, blow-up figures, and everything in-between. The place was a true tribute to the Griswolds from National Lampoon's Christmas Vacation. He paused there, staring from his car window at the spectacle.

"Do you see what I see?" I mumbled.

"A star dancing in the night?"

I swerved my head toward him, instantly

picking up on his Christmas song reference. "We've been hanging around for way too long." I pointed to the decorations just as Benjamin pulled away. "That's the house he's going to hit tonight." I nodded confidently as hope surged in me.

"I have to admit. That did seem eerie. You could be right."

I glanced over at Chad. "We've got to be there to catch him."

***

"This was not what I thought you had in mind." Chad turned toward me and scowled, the expression obvious despite the big white beard covering his face.

I readjusted my halo and smiled. "I think this is perfect."

Tucked beneath the folds of my angel dress was a camera so I could snap pictures as evidence. I also had on a coat with my cell phone in the pocket, just in case. I'd invited Riley, but he had practice for the Living Christmas Tree.

Earlier, Chad and I had paid a visit to Wanda, the homeowner. She was in her forties, plump with curly brown hair, and had the biggest eyes I'd ever seen. We explained about the other homes that had been vandalized. Her mouth had dropped open in horror. She'd agreed that we could set up our "sting" operation in hopes of catching the culprit.

Since the woman had some life-sized mannequins displayed in her front yard, we blended right in . . . when we could stay still, at least. The cold made my nose run and my eyes water. We'd been standing here for an hour already. A line of cars had continuously driven past. This house was probably a yearly tradition for many spectators wanting something obnoxious to gawk at. I wondered if Jesus ever imagined his birth would turn into something like this. I wondered if it pleased or disappointed him.

There I went, thinking about Jesus like he was real. But maybe he was. Why was I being so resistant to the idea right now?

Soon, the owner would turn off the lights and "retire" for the night. That's when the culprit would strike.

Chad remained still and only moved his lips—just as I'd instructed him. "Couldn't we have just stayed in the car for the same effect?"

"It wouldn't have been nearly as much fun. Plus, he might have seen the van and recognized it."

Suddenly, everything went dark. I saw the curtain move, and Wanda waved 'okay' to us. I nodded back to her. We told her not to come out and talk to us, just in case someone was watching.

We didn't want to blow our cover.

Without the lights on, everything seemed spookier, like we were in some kind of Christmas ghost town.

The minutes ticked by. The wind caused the branches of some nearby trees to clack together. The full moon above us seemed like an omen of bad things to come. Pine needles on a nearby evergreen swished together, almost as if nature was whispering about us.

Then everything got quiet. Too quiet?

Movement in the side yard caught my eye. My heart sped as perspiration sprinkled across my forehead. What was that? A deranged killer planning a sneak attack?

A screech cut through the air. My scream caught in my throat as I jumped toward Chad. My hands trembled as I grasped his arm. "What was that?"

Chad pointed in the distance, a smile pulling at his lips. "A cat. Just a cat."

Just then, I saw the feline's eyes glowing green from the grove of pine trees. It wasn't just a cat, either. It was a black cat. I let out an airy laugh and released my death grip on Chad. I brushed myself off and raised my chin, acting like I'd known the whole time. "Of course."

I realized that Chad was right—this was a

bad idea. My legs hurt, my skin felt like it had a layer of frost on it, and I wondered if Benjamin Videl was even going to show up here tonight at all.

Chad kept himself entertained by singing the Twelve Days of Christmas. I chuckled uneasily under my breath as he tried desperately to think of what objects went with the numbers. Eleven chicks a dancing? Seven sluggers slugging? I couldn't do much better.

Of course, the way my thoughts were going didn't take me down the entertainment route. No, I was thinking about Five Golden Teeth, Four Strands of Hair, Three Crime Scenes, Two Sitting Ducks, and the Ear of a Dead Wise Man.

My bones felt brittle from the cold, but my nerves felt even more brittle as the minutes ticked by. At midnight—I'd just checked my watch a few minutes earlier—a car swerved into the driveway.

I braced myself, ready to run in case the car kept going and tried to run us over. The driver slammed on the brakes and cut his headlights. My shoulders loosened some—but only temporarily.

I stared at the car. It was a dark color. Black maybe? Black, as in, Benjamin Videl's car?

I tried to remain perfectly still, but more than anything, I wanted to glance at Chad, to exchange "that look" that proved we were onto something.

I couldn't believe Benjamin had pulled into

the driveway. Didn't he have more sense than that? It seemed awfully brazen to me.

He climbed from the car, a bag slung over his shoulder. My throat went dry at the sight. What was in that bag? A head? A hand? Some other kind of decomposing body part?

His gaze scanned the life-sized decorations in front of the house. What was he planning? A bombing? At least he hadn't run us over—yet.

I could see the confusion on his face as he paced through the front yard, examining each of the figures there. That's when my nerves starting tightening. Examining each of the figures? That was definitely not something I'd planned on. I figured the person behind these acts simply came, did their deed, and left.

I tried not to breathe. I knew my breath would be frosty in front of me. But how long could I hold my breath without passing out? That remained to be seen.

The man was clearly Benjamin. We'd been right.

He reached into his pocket and pulled out a . . . lighter? Was he planning to burn this down? He walked right toward Chad and me.

I could feel myself turning blue from lack of air. I couldn't hold my breath much longer, and some psycho just might be planning on setting me on fire.

He got closer, that lighter extended out in front of him.

Suddenly, Santa-Chad burst to life. "No!" Chad yelled before tackling Ben the Mortician.

Benjamin dropped everything and began flailing his hands in the air and screaming like a girl as Chad pinned him on the ground.

Had we just single-handedly saved Christmas?

So it appeared.

Just then, all the lights came on. Wanda scrambled from the house, her phone in hand, and her eyes wide with worry. "Did you catch him? Did you catch the man behind this?"

Chad stood, half of his beard now wrapped around the side of his face. He pulled Benjamin up by his coat. "We sure did. And it's all thanks to you."

Wanda gasped, lunging forward and swatting at Chad. "Let go of him!"

"Why would we do that? He tried to set us on fire!" I tried to hold her back, tried to protect my friend from the mayhem. The woman was stronger than I thought, especially when she elbowed me in the gut before scrambling toward Benjamin.

"Because this man's my husband! He put up all of these Christmas decorations."

Chapter 8

Police Navidad

I sat in Benjamin Videl's house, along with Chad whom I'd pulled into this mess. He wasn't very happy with me. I couldn't blame him either. He could be facing assault charges and both of us could be charged with trespassing. I wondered what Riley would say if I asked him to post bail or represent us?

"Ms. St. Claire, you have some explaining to do or I will be calling the police." Benjamin Videl narrowed his eyes at me.

I dug my hands into the upholstered sofa, finally deciding to sit on my fingers in an effort to regain feeling in my frozen digits. "It's like I told you. I followed you and saw you drive past this house today. You lingered outside for long enough that I got suspicious."

"I'm allowed to drive past my own house!" Benjamin nearly came out of his seat, lunging toward me with fury glowing in his eyes.

I held up my hands, prepared to defend

myself both physically and verbally if need be. "You didn't even go inside! You just lingered outside on the street in your car. That's called suspicious in my book."

"I wanted to make sure all of the lights and figures were working properly! I knew I wouldn't be getting home until late tonight because my part-timer called in sick again." He pointed toward his front yard. "This is what I love to do. I add to my Christmas collection every year. I've made the newspaper with my light shows. I love Christmas. I don't want to destroy it!"

I bit my lip. I'd really messed up this time, hadn't I?

"Why would you think my husband was guilty in the first place?" Wanda waited for my response. She stood between us like a referee. Only I'd been the one who'd been stuck with a penalty.

Chad cleared his throat, still drowning in his Santa costume. "We narrowed down a list of possible morticians in the area who might be guilty."

"Using what criteria?"

I cringed. "The creep factor?"

"Ms. St. Claire—"

I raised my hands. "I know. I know! I messed up, and I truly am sorry."

And I was truly certain I would never, ever

live this one down.

***

Thankfully, the Videls hadn't pressed charges. I had to give them credit for that. They had said something, however, about never wanting to see me within fifty feet of them again. I couldn't imagine why.

As we left, my cell phone buzzed. It was Pastor Shaggy. "We've got another vandalism."

"Where? What?"

"Some farm animals from a living nativity are missing."

Animals? I knew just the person who could help with this.

Standing in the front yard of a little farmhouse in Virginia Beach, I took stock of my surroundings. The properties on this lonely stretch of road were spaced far and wide. In the back of the yard was a huge barn and somewhere a sheep bleated and a cow mooed. Police officers, the family who owned the place, and Detective Adams murmured not too far away. Other than that, the area was encased in somewhat of a country silence, void of the sounds of highways and teenagers roaming the neighborhood and college football games. In other words, it was the total opposite of where I lived.

I jammed my hands—still frozen after the fiasco at the Videls' place—into my coat pockets and allowed my gaze to peruse the front lawn. A Christmas tree stand stood at one side of the yard and a huge, life-sized nativity on the other. It was probably a true sight-to-see when there were live people and animals filling the space.

I knew that people came to buy their trees, sip some hot apple cider, and ponder the living nativity. I couldn't be certain, but in the back of my mind, I felt like I'd been here before. Had my mom brought me when I was little? I couldn't be sure.

A few minutes ago, I'd overheard that the police had found a note reading, *Police Navidad.* Appropriate since law enforcement would be involved.

Not only that, but now that song was going to be stuck in my head all day.

I rubbed my arms, wondering what body part had been left at this scene. Speaking of which, I had to get that tooth and those vials to Detective Adams also. Guilt clawed at me.

Detective Adams finally came up to us, and I hoped he'd feel generous enough to fill us in.

"Ms. St. Claire." He scowled.

"Did you find a body part?"

"That's information that only the authorities

are privy to."

"Oh, come on. Just a little hint? Can you blink once for yes, twice for no?"

He stared at me, unblinking, until I crossed my arms.

"Fine," I mumbled.

"What about the animals?" Sierra stepped forward, pushing her plastic framed glasses up higher on her nose. Her normally silky black hair was matted on one side. I'd obviously woken her up and she'd obviously jumped out of bed to come here when she'd heard about the urgency of the situation. That was Sierra for you. Don't mess with animals.

He sucked in a deep breath. "A sheep is missing."

"A sheep? Someone stole a sheep and expects to get away with it?" Sierra's fisted hands went to her tiny hips.

Detective Adams nodded slowly, like he was biting his tongue tonight. "They were in the barn. The owners had heard a commotion, but by the time they got outside, the sheep was gone and taillights were flashing in the distance.

What in the world would someone do with a farm animal?

"They stole a sheep!" Sierra repeated, still shaking her head. "These people are going to be caught. I'll make sure of it."

A smile started to curl my lip. "How are you going to do that?"

"I have a great network of animal lovers who will be on the lookout. Don't worry. I'll get to the bottom of this."

I had no doubt she would.

***

The next morning, I picked up a pen and a piece of paper as I sat at my kitchen table with a mug of coffee. The day outside was overcast—it almost looked like we could have snow. Wouldn't that be perfect to add to everyone's idea of what the ideal Christmas looked like? I had to admit that the idea secretly made me feel warm and cozy. But as I looked across the room at my Charlie Brown Christmas tree that I'd propped up in one of my cleaning buckets, I realized my Christmas was anything but warm and cozy.

Tonight was the Christmas parade through Ghent, and I'd promised my friends I would go with them. Ms. Holiday Cheer, remember? I had to admit that all these Christmas songs and traditions were beginning to grow on me. And the idea of a White Christmas had its appeal. Maybe I could get into the Christmas spirit this year after all. I should give it a shot.

I shoved those Winter Wonderland thoughts aside to focus on the task at hand: writing a suspect list. Yep, I would make my list and check it twice.

Marvin Harris was the first name I jotted. He was the man behind the Coalition Against Christmas. But was his fight purely intellectual?

Oliver Nichols was next. He hated Christmas also, but he claimed he would never do something like this. I still couldn't help but think that this would give him some great publicity—if he wasn't caught.

Benjamin Videl was next on my list. I guess he'd been officially cleared after the debacle last night, but someone was getting those embalmed body parts from somewhere. Besides, rearrange the letters of his last name and you had the word "Devil." Coincidence? Maybe his whole "I love Christmas" thing was just an act to cover up his true feelings.

I sighed, realizing I had nothing solid to go on. I glanced at my pen again as I tapped it against my paper. That's when it hit me.

I knew where I'd seen the Videl Funeral Home logo before. Mrs. Claus at the costume shop was using a pen with that logo across it when we went into her shop.

It looked like I was going to be paying her

another visit.

I glanced at my watch. Right after I finished cleaning a crime scene.

***

Mrs. Claus scowled when I walked into her establishment. Based on the way she turned up her nose, she definitely recognized me. Or maybe it was because I hadn't had time to go home and shower after cleaning that crime scene. After a while, you became numb to the scent of blood that saturated your skin and hair. Even with the Hazmat suit I wore, the smell could still claim you.

"I still don't have any answers for you. Many people have purchased or rented Santa Claus costumes over the past couple of days, and no, I won't release their names." She straightened some papers—rather loudly, I might add—before huffing and staring at me.

"That's not why I'm here."

"Then please do tell why. I'm very busy, as you can see."

The shop was actually void of customers, but I didn't bring that up. "What's your association with the Videl Funeral Home?"

"Videl? Why would you think I'm associated with them?"

"You were using their pen the other day when we came in."

"Is that a crime?"

"Of course not. I'm just trying to connect the dots."

She leaned toward me. "Let me get this straight. The funeral home is now behind the slaying of Christmas spirit around town?"

I shook my head. "I didn't say that. I'm just trying to find some answers. Your lack of cooperation makes you look guilty of hiding something."

"I'm not hiding anything, young lady, and I resent your implications. I can use whatever pen I please."

"I realize that. I'm just trying to figure out where you got it. Is that too much to ask?"

She leaned toward me, anger flashing in her eyes. "My sister works there. Are you happy now?"

I pulled back and nodded. Another dead end? I couldn't be sure. "Thanks for your help and for being forthcoming."

"Please, don't come back unless you plan on purchasing something. The sign on the door says 'No Soliciting,' and that includes soliciting information on crimes. Got it?"

"Oh, I've got it alright."

I shook my head as I walked outside. Some

people . . .

A glance at my watch told me I had just enough time to change and get ready for the Christmas parade. Pastor Shaggy and Charity had planned the event.

Why did a sense of foreboding seem to settle between my shoulders at the thought?

Chapter 9

Slashing Through the Snow

"Are those actually protesters?" I pointed to a group at the start of the parade who were holding picket signs. "Don't people have anything better to do?"

Riley shook his head, his lips twisted in disgust. "Apparently not."

"This isn't a war on Christmas. This is a war on everything merry and bright." I nodded toward a familiar face in the crowd. "There's Marvin Harris, head of the Coalition Against Christmas. I guess they're behind this spectacle. They're literally trying to rain on the parade."

"They're behind a lot of spectacles," Riley muttered. "But I'm not going to think about them tonight. I'm going to think about having a good time."

We'd already seen fire engines and antique cars. A couple of dance troupes came past, as well as two marching bands. Pastor Shaggy and his Operation: Save Christmas had a float they'd put together to promote The Living Christmas Tree.

I shivered, trying to enjoy myself. That was hard to do when all you could think about was that something bad could happen here. This would be the perfect place.

I glanced around. Chad and Sierra were buying some hot chocolate for all of us down at a little stand set up by some elementary kids. Families lined the streets. People had brought their pets, or animal companions as Sierra called them.

If I let my guard down, I just might enjoy this parade. But letting my guard down was so hard. I might even let myself enjoy Christmas. The problem with getting your hopes up was that when those same hopes were dashed, it could set you back even farther than before.

"It's a nice look on you." Riley tapped the bells springing from the headband atop my head. Chad had brought it for me. I'd have to think of a way to thank him later. Maybe I'd bring him a "I love the Kardashians" T-Shirt. Yes, something utterly disgraceful and embarrassing.

I pointed down the row of parade floats. "Here they come now."

Pastor Shaggy had designed a float full of angels singing heavenly choruses alongside a living nativity that even had two sheep munching on some grass beside the shepherds. I really hoped Sierra didn't see them and jump into action. I recognized Charity as one of the angels standing along the perimeter. Her gaze was focused on Pastor Shaggy, who was dressed as one of the Wise Men.

I squinted. What was wrong with that float? Something was off.

I blinked. That was it. The fence that stretched around the float had a little gate to the side. The door fluttered open with the breeze.

The next thing I knew, one of the sheep jumped off. The creature began running through the crowds, causing screams and some nervous laughter to scatter throughout the crowd as two men began chasing it. The entire back end of the parade came to a stop.

A loud "neigh" sounded. I jerked my head toward the noise just in time to see one of the stallions from the Pungo Equestrian Club rear back on two legs. The rider tried to rein the brown stallion in, but the horse continued to panic. He rose up on his hind legs, nostrils flaring in fear. The other horses around him began to scatter as their riders tried to bring them under control.

Screams sliced the air as people ran for cover. People in the back craned their necks, searching for the source of danger crackling through the air. The stallion neighed and rose up on two feet again.

My eyes zeroed in on a little boy, probably only five, who stood under the horse, his eyes wide. Someone had to help that boy. Where were his parents?

Nowhere to be seen. Everyone just stared in horror.

I darted toward him just as the horse reared back again. He let out a little cry. I dove until my hands could push him. He flew out of the way, and Riley grabbed him.

But not before the horse's feet came down on my back. Pain rushed through me and lights flashed in my eyes.

The last thing I remembered was Riley yelling, "Gabby!"

Then I closed my eyes and let the darkness swallow me.

***

Three hours later, Riley drove me home from the hospital. He'd done this a couple of times already, so it almost seemed like a routine. I get hurt, Riley helps me out, and then we argue over how much rest I should get to help accelerate the healing process.

I had a bruised rib, but it could have been so much worse.

At least it hadn't been the little boy.

Somehow the gate on that parade float had come unlatched, the sheep had gotten out, and the horse had gotten spooked. Some people said it was a coincidence. I knew it wasn't. Someone had tampered with the gate, knowing it would open and cause mayhem. The question was who?

I stared out the window as we drove down the very street where the parade had taken place. How could such a pleasant night have turned into this? "So much for peace on earth and goodwill to men," I muttered. I snapped my gaze up to Riley. "Didn't mean to say that aloud. Again. I've gotta stop doing that."

He reached over and squeezed my hand. "I should have grabbed you, Gabby."

I shook my head. "No, you should have grabbed the boy. You did the right thing."

"I should have grabbed both of you."

"That would have been impossible. It's better that the horse landed on me. He would have crushed that little boy."

"His parents were thankful. They were chasing their three year old, who was chasing the sheep."

A few more blocks rolled by in silence. But Riley didn't drop my hand. I tried not to notice or care. But it didn't work. Finally, we pulled up to the apartment. Riley's hand slipped from mine, and he ran around to my side of the car to open the door for me. Gently, he helped me out of the car. His hand remained on my elbow as we went inside. Each step was painful. Each breath felt painful, for that matter.

"You've got to rest tonight and take it easy," Riley reminded me as we started up the steps. "That could have been much worse."

"Haven't we been through this before?"

Riley paused at my doorstep. What was that look in his eyes? Those beautiful blue eyes. "Way too many times."

I pushed a hair behind my ear, the bandage around my mid-section making me feel like I'd put on twenty pounds—twenty painful pounds.

He paused and stared at me a moment like he wanted to say something. Instead, he shoved his hands into his pockets and nodded. "You going to be okay?"

"Always." I offered a winning grin.

He slipped my hospital bracelet off and handed it to me with a sad smile. "I'll see you in the morning."

I slipped into my apartment and collapsed onto the sofa. I was so exhausted that I didn't even have time to dwell on the goodbye and the what-could-have or might-have-been. Instead, I took my prescribed pain medication and slept.

***

Knocking woke me up.

Who in the world was knocking at my door in the middle of the night?

I pulled my eyes open and realized that it was daylight outside. A glance at my digital clock told me it was nearly noon. Wow, I really had been tired.

"Gabby? You okay in there?"

Riley. Of course, it was Riley. The ever-concerned neighbor and Christian. The one who treated me with brotherly love.

Not exactly what I wanted, but I supposed that I'd take what I could get.

"Coming," I mumbled, pulling myself into sitting position. I didn't even want to think about what my hair might look like. On a good day, it looked like a wreck—red, springy curls exploding all around my face. Today, I could only imagine the atrocity that would be considered my hair.

I stood—I tried to, at least. My ribs felt like an elephant had crushed them. No, it had just been a horse instead.

"Gabby?"

"Really, I'm coming. Slowly."

Finally, I managed to stand. Holding onto the back of the couch for balance, I crept toward the door, opened it, and then collapsed into the nearest chair.

"Are you okay?" Those beautiful, concerned eyes met mine again.

"I think I need to take more pain medicine."

"Tell me where you left it, and I'll grab it for you."

I told him, and a moment later, he was kneeling by me with a pill in one hand and a glass of water in the other. I took the medicine, knowing it would take a few minutes for it to kick in.

"You look . . . "

I popped an eye open, waiting for him to finish. Daring him to finish, maybe I should say.

"Like you're in pain," he finally said.

"I look rough. Just say it. I know it's true."

"Do I look stupid? I know better than to tell a woman that."

I smiled, my arm still wrapped around my rib cage. "What happened last night? Did Pastor Shaggy tell you? Because I know something happened. A vandalism a day keeps the Christmas cheer away."

"This one will surprise you."

I actually forgot about my pain for a moment. "Then do tell."

"Someone broke into the mall and spray-painted the Pictures with Santa area."

"That doesn't have anything to do with Jesus."

He nodded. "I know. Apparently, this is truly a war on Christmas as a whole and not just the religious aspect of the holiday." His face twisted. "I just said holiday, and now I feel guilty."

"I'm sure God will forgive you." I offered my best grin, which wasn't much. "Body part?"

"An eyeball."

"An eyeball?"

"Yeah, it had been replaced in one of the figures beside Santa. There are tons of video cameras at the mall, but again the man just looked like Santa."

"How'd he get in?"

"Apparently, based on what the police found on the security cameras, this person hid in the bathroom after the mall closed. Once everyone cleared out, he vandalized the Santa area and escaped out a back exit. The police are wondering if maybe it was an inside job since the suspect knew about the back entrance. The alarm went off when the vandal left, but he was long gone by the time security got there."

"Song?" I asked, wondering what musical number the note referenced this time.

"The note said, 'The Crime that Stole

Christmas.'"

"Interesting."

"There's one more thing. Charity told me she found a box from the M. H. Company with a snake inside at the parade last night, right in the same area where that horse got spooked."

I sat up straighter. "A box with a snake?"

"Does that ring a bell?"

"Marvin Harris owns a box company, and he's a snake enthusiast. That can't be a coincidence. Plus, he was the person who showed up at the pastor's house, and that was right before he got hurt. I have to let Detective Adams know."

"Sounds like a good idea." Riley handed me the phone. Luckily, I knew the detective's number by heart. He asked me how I was doing, and I shared the news with him, waiting for the moment where he thanked me profusely for putting two-and-two together.

"We have a lead we're following. We're closing in, you could say."

I stared at my empty Christmas tree and scowled. "You have another suspect?"

"We do. And we don't need you interfering with our investigation, Ms. St. Claire."

How could he have another lead? What had I missed? I thanked him, hung up, and relayed the information to Riley.

Riley leaned against the kitchen counter and nodded. "By the way, Chad's on his way up."

I noticed the change of subject but chose not to address it. I didn't have the energy. "Why?"

"We're going to make fruitcake."

"Fruitcake? Why in the world would we make that?"

"What better way to torture people at Christmastime? At least, I believe that was the way Chad put it. Anyway, we're going to give them out tonight at Sierra's Ugly Christmas Sweater Party."

The Ugly Christmas Sweater Party. I'd nearly forgotten.

Maybe that would take my mind off crime and help me focus a little more on Christmas.

Chapter 10

Mopping Around the Christmas Tree

I was thankful to say that I had to purchase my ugly Christmas sweater at a thrift store and that I didn't already have one on hand. I was also thankful that I'd purchased it a couple of weeks ago, and that it was big enough to cover the bandages at my ribs.

With a giant Christmas tree across the front—decorated with bells and little plaid bows, I might add—I blended right in with all of the other tacky attire at Sierra's Ugly Christmas Sweater party. But I had to admit that I was having a hard time getting into the holiday spirit. Christmas was only three days away and I still hadn't caught the person behind these crimes.

As Riley and I lingered near the doorway at her party, I spotted various coworkers of Sierra's from Paws and Fur Balls milling around the apartment, as well as Chad and radio talk show host Bill McCormick. I couldn't help but notice the brochures Sierra had also strategically placed around her apartment, probably trying to convert some people into being vegan. She was passionate about what she did. I'd give her that.

As soon as Sierra spotted me, she charged my way. She wore a red and green checkered Christmas vest over the most obnoxious reindeer T-shirt I've ever seen. Score one for my animal loving friend.

"You'll never believe this." Her eyes sparkled. "I sent out word to all of my friends about the missing sheep. A couple of hours ago, we got a call about the sheep, so one of my friends went out to investigate. You'll never believe this—they found it!"

I knew that this news was like a Christmas present to her. To me too, for that matter. "They did? Where?"

Her hand flew through the air. "It turns out the homeowner is some anti-Christmas guy. His name is Oliver Nichols."

"Oliver Nichols?" I nearly choked.

"You know him?"

I shrugged. "I guess you could say that."

"He lives in a subdivision. All things considered, it was a really stupid place to try and hide a sheep of all things. He claims he was out of town and that the police were at his house when he arrived back home."

Exactly. He was smarter than that. Had

someone set him up?

Sierra grabbed my arms, nearly jumping with joy. "Isn't that fabulous news? You can finally enjoy Christmas!"

I tried to smile. I really did. And I did want to enjoy Christmas.

So why did I find it so hard to believe that Oliver Nichols was behind this? He appeared to have some anger issues. He had an obvious hatred of the holiday. The vandalisms were great publicity for his book. So my doubts made no sense.

Riley leaned close—close enough that shivers raced down my arm. "You okay?"

I nodded. "Yeah, of course. Just sore."

"Maybe you should sit down."

Maybe you shouldn't act like you care so much. I didn't say it aloud, but I wanted to. Would my heart ever leave this state of turmoil when I was around Riley? I sat and tried to dispel my thoughts as the evening went on.

The night was fun, complete with a fashion show. Sierra even had everyone make Christmas ornaments that they then gifted me with. I'd finally have something to decorate my tree! Sharon, from The Grounds, dropped by some sugar cookies in the shape of ugly Christmas sweaters, of course. Sierra had questioned her intensely to make sure they were free of eggs and other animal byproducts before allowing her to come in. Meanwhile, the rest of us partygoers had been drooling, ready for some real food and not just the vegan variety. The fruitcakes had already been banned—not that anyone had wanted to eat them.

Despite the holiday festivities, my heart remained nearly as heavy as my thoughts.

I had to put this case behind me.

Why was that easier said than done?

***

The morning dawned bright and cheery. Or maybe that was because it was almost noon. Again.

On Christmas Eve Eve.

A small flutter of excitement whipped through me as I eased myself out of bed. The bad guy was behind bars—if law enforcement had gotten it right, at least—and tonight was the Living Christmas Tree.

Everything should be smooth sailing from here on out . . . right? So why did I still feel that familiar knot of apprehension?

It was just my imagination, I told myself.

It took almost all of my energy to make myself some toast for breakfast. Then I went to the Christmas tree and placed each of the goofy ornaments that my friends had made me on the branches.

I stepped back and looked at the finished product. Not bad. Not bad at all, for a Charlie Brown Christmas tree. I'd been too exhausted when I arrived home from the party last night to decorate. But seeing the tree filled with miniature ugly sweaters caused a sense of satisfaction to rise in me.

A single girl could still have a great Christmas. It was a matter of choice. Charity had said so, and if Charity could have a good Christmas after everything she'd been through, then so could I.

I'd bought a few presents—including a new computer modem for myself—right after Thanksgiving. Today, I'd spend the day wrapping those gifts and listening to Christmas music. Later I'd brave the elements and my ribs in order to go to the Living Christmas Tree.

Most of all, I'd try to celebrate the case of Mr. Scrooge finally being solved. But *try* was the key word because I still wasn't 100 percent convinced. Maybe it was the pain meds. Maybe I was just bored. Why couldn't I let go of the idea that a crazed body part snatcher lurked unchecked?

Three hours later, Riley chauffeured me to Towne Point Park in downtown Norfolk. It was a quaint little park located on the Elizabeth River. From where I stood, I could see the Battleship

Wisconsin—an older destroyer that was now open for the public to tour—as well as a waterfront museum called Nauticus.

Riley opened a red camping chair for me and instructed me to sit. I wanted to argue, but I couldn't. Sitting sounded really nice. I looked up at him—he wore a Kelly green sweater with a striped red and green scarf around his neck. No tights or elf ears, however. "Someone did check out the area where you're standing to make sure it hasn't been tampered with, right?"

"The person behind everything has been arrested, Gabby. Oliver Nichols is in custody. It's been all over the news."

I pressed my lips together, unable to come to peace with the information. "He hasn't confessed. I talked to Pastor Shaggy earlier, and he's been in contact with some of the homeowners who are pressing charges, so he knows the scoop on everything."

"A lot of criminals don't confess. Stop worrying so much. He sent nasty letters to the church and to the mall. He also has a brother-in-law who works for a funeral home up in Northern Virginia. He's our guy." Someone in the distance called him, and he took a step back. "Look, I've got to run and get ready to sing. Are you going to be okay?"

I nodded. As he hurried to join the rest of the choir, I leaned back in my chair and looked up at the wooden structure built in the shape of a Christmas tree. Within the structure were five different levels of platforms where the choir would stand to sing. Wreaths, garland, and evergreen branches decorated the structure. It was really beautiful. I had to admit that.

A crowd gathered, most of them dressed in scarves and mittens and knit hats. A bitterly cold wind swept across the river, bringing with it a few flecks of icy precipitation. Snow, maybe?

Man, this would be the perfect moment for something to go wrong.

I shook my head, which probably made me look like the crazy lady who talked to herself, but I didn't care. Still, I couldn't think like that. The person behind those vandalisms was behind bars. Leave it to me to always look for a mystery in the middle of something.

My gaze scanned the crowds. I half expected Marvin Harris to show up picketing again. After all, this was being held on public property. Instead of seeing Marvin Harris, I spotted another familiar face, though. Warren—the ex-drug addict who'd taken the holy family hostage atop his house.

He attends Pastor Shaggy's church, I reminded myself. So naturally he was here to support the pastor and not for more sinister reasons. Still, my guard remained up.

Thirty minutes later, just as the sun dipped below the horizon, an area-wide choir emerged in line formation and filled the Christmas tree. From a small stage up front, Pastor Shaggy announced them as a choir director took her place. Everyone quieted as "O Christmas Tree" began to waft across the park. My mind wandered to everything that had happened. What was I missing?

What traits did my gut tell me the perpetrator had?

A bad childhood memory of Christmas.
Psycho.

Access to body parts at a funeral home through their job.

Psycho.

Privy to everything going on, including where Pastor Shaggy lived.

Psycho.

Knowledgeable enough to make a bomb.

One face appeared in my mind. My heart sped at the thought.

No. It couldn't be. I shook my head again.

But I'd bet it was.

My eyes scanned the crowd. Was that person here? Just what dastardly deed had the psycho planned for tonight?

I spotted Santa, the person I was looking for from across the way. Here. At the Living Christmas Tree. I stood, my ribs screaming with enough pain that I winced. I had to reach this person before it was too late.

The choir began "Silent Night."

My number one suspect disappeared behind the Christmas tree, and my worst fears were confirmed. Something bad was going down tonight. I had to do something. Now.

I paused in front of the tree and began waving my arms at the crowd. "Stop everything!" I yelled. "Get back!"

People could barely hear me over the music blaring from the speakers on either side of me. Where was Pastor Shaggy? I had to find him.

My arm wrapped around my rib cage as pain ripped through me. I had to push through that. Finally, I saw the pastor. I lumbered toward him and gripped his arm. "You've got to clear the area out. Something bad is going to happen."

"What?" He cupped his hand around his ear.

This silent night wasn't so silent. "Something bad is going to happen!" I screamed.

Just then, the music cut. Everyone stared at me. I looked up at Riley, perched on the top of the tree like the angel he was. "You've got to get down! Now!"

Finally, my words seemed to sink in. People began scrambling down. Good, because I didn't have time to wait around here. "Help them," I shouted to Shaggy.

I looked back up at Riley. He tried to tell me something, but I couldn't understand what. There was no time to waste. I had to find the person responsible for these crimes before a lot of people got hurt.

Jesus, help them.

I didn't pray often. But in my distress, the possibility of Jesus seemed like the greatest possibility of all times.

Probably because it was. That's what Riley would say, at least.

As fast as my ribs allowed me to move, I ran until I reached the area behind the Christmas tree. In the distance, I saw Santa disappear behind a row of port-a-johns placed near the docks. I pushed myself harder.

Just as I rounded the corner, something slammed into my head. Pain screamed from my temples, and my vision burred as I fell to the ground.

Santa's face appeared.

Or should I say, Charity's. Charity with a fake beard.

Gone was her sweet innocence. It had been

replaced with vengeance.

"Goodbye, Ms. St. Claire," she said in a singsong voice.

She stomped on my ribs before rolling me away from the port-a-johns—and right toward the river.

I had to stop rolling. If I hit that ice-cold water in my current state, I'd be a goner. No way could I swim. I could barely breathe.

I clawed at the cement pavers lining the port and managed to drag myself to my knees. The tip of Charity's boot collided with my ribs again. Tears rushed to my eyes as pain ripped through my midsection.

She shoved me again, and I braced myself for an ice-cold death.

***

"Charity, stop!"

My head may have been aching, but I was pretty sure I'd heard someone. Pastor Shaggy.

Charity paused, looking back quickly before glaring down at me.

"Don't do it, Charity," the pastor said. He huffed and puffed as he came to stop in front of us. "We're going to help you work through this. You don't have to hurt anyone else."

"I want everyone to hurt, just like I hurt. You wouldn't understand." She had crazy eyes, and her voice had gone up an octave. This was a woman who'd already lost it—she'd just covered it up too well for too long.

I gripped my ribs and tried to get a deep breath. Breathing hurt horrendously bad. But I had to get up. I had to do something before she focused all of her fury on me and the rest of the world again.

Standing was useless, so I began to crawl back toward the grass.

Charity looked back at me, a deadly sparkle gleaming in her eyes. She pulled out a gun from beneath her fur-trimmed Santa jacket and pointed it at me. "Not so fast."

The pastor raised his hands toward her in peace. "Charity, stop this. Now."

Her nostrils flared, and she cocked the little black pistol. "I might as well finish what I started. I'm going to jail anyway."

He stepped closer. "I want to help you."

Charity narrowed her eyes, not softened at all to his gestures of friendship. "You want to help everyone, don't you?"

Movement behind the port-a-john caught my eye. Riley? Was that really Riley? He was okay. Praise Jesus, he was okay.

Charity turned toward me, the gun pointed at

my chest. All the moisture disappeared from my mouth. This was it—the moment I was going to die. The moment I'd meet my maker. My blood froze at the thought.

Jesus, help me!

A gun fired just as Riley dove in front of me.

***

Riley had been shot.

Oh no. Riley had been shot. How could Riley have been shot?

Panic raced through me. I screamed until my ribs felt like they were being torn out of me.

Riley . . .

I tried to lift my head, but the weight of his body as he covered me made it nearly impossible.

Jesus, help him. You saved the world. Save Riley.

Just then, Riley moved. His head slowly rose.

I studied his face, wondering if I was seeing things.

His eyes looked dazed, and there was a cut on his forehead. But he was still here. Riley was still here. "You're alive!"

He wiped a hair out of my eyes. "Of course I'm alive. Are you okay?"

I nodded, my arm still wrapped around my

rib cage. "Thanks to you." He'd been willing to take a bullet for me, and that was something that I would never, ever forget. He sat up and pulled my head into his lap.

"I don't want to move you until the medics are here."

That was fine, because I had no desire to move. Every part of my body ached. "Who fired that gun?"

Detective Adams stepped forward, his gun going back into the holster at his shoulders. He'd fired, not Charity. I looked over and saw Charity clutching her hand as pain twisted her features. Pastor Shaggy kicked her gun out of the way and knelt beside her.

I glanced up at the detective, my entire body rebelling at any movement. "How'd you know?"

He motioned for another officer to arrest Charity before coming to my side. "Gut feeling. Those other clues implicating Oliver Nichols just seemed to come to light too easily. The question is how did you know?

"I remembered her talking about working a part-time job. I also remembered Benjamin Videl saying that his part-time employee kept showing up late, if at all. Her tragic Christmas background gave her motive. She teaches high school chemistry so she would know how to make a bomb. She could

have easily let that sheep off of the parade float. Everything finally came together and made sense."

He patted my hand. "Good job. Again." He glanced over his shoulder. "The medics are here. They'll take a look at you. You're one brave woman, Gabby St. Claire. You saved a lot of lives tonight."

I nodded. But there was one person who'd saved mine. Riley Thomas.

Chapter 11

It's a Wonderful Epilogue

"Christmas is just one time of the year when we can pay honor to Jesus," Pastor Shaggy said to the crowds around the dark Christmas tree structure in the park. They all gathered around him, their candles pushing away the darkness, as he told the Christmas story. "God became man because he loved us. God's Son died because he loved us. No matter what senseless violence occurs, or the heartbreaks, or the pain, Jesus is the one person who will never let us down."

I liked the sound of that.

Pastor Shaggy continued by telling the crowds that we were made for more than the bickering, made for more than living for ourselves, made for more than revenge or misery. We were made in love, and we were here to love.

I liked the idea that someone would give his life for me—just like Riley almost had. The Greatest Story Ever Told was beginning to grow on me, and I had some big decisions to make soon.

Maybe some of Riley's goodness and optimism was beginning to rub off on me.

The crowds around Pastor Shaggy began to sing "Joy to the World." I smiled and clicked off the TV, where they had been running the news story over and over for the past day.

Right now, Riley and I sat on my couch, taking it easy for once.

I looked up at him. He was decked out in a black sweater and looked so sophisticated and handsome. I was so grateful to have him in my life.

"I'd say Charity's plan backfired big time," he started. "The support has been overwhelming. Even organizations that you would expect to be against us have come forward to say that everything that happened was atrocious."

"That's awesome." My smile slipped into a frown. "I know this sounds weird, but I feel bad for Charity."

"The pastor is making sure she gets the help she needs."

I didn't want to be like Charity. I didn't want to let my past make me bitter or, in her case, deranged. I was going to make a choice to be joy-filled this Christmas.

Riley stood. "I should be getting home."

"Thanks for everything, Riley."

He smiled down at me. "I have a lot to thank

you for, too. You saved a lot of people tonight. Charity had planted another bomb under that tree."

Even though Riley tried to stop me, I stood also. The pain medication helped my ribs, but they still ached. Of course, they didn't ache as much as my heart did when I thought about what Riley had done for me. "By the way, Detective Adams said he got the results back on those vials and the tooth."

"You gave them to him?"

"Of course I did. A couple of days ago, actually. It was the legal thing to do."

He quirked an eyebrow. "And?"

"The tooth belonged to the same person as the hair. The first liquid was formaldehyde, just as I guessed. Charity told the police that the second liquid was . . . tears."

"Tears?"

I nodded. "Probably Charity's way of trying to let people know just how sad she really is. And it is sad."

He reached into his pocket and pulled out a small box. "Merry Christmas, by the way."

"For me?"

He nodded.

I tore away the gold paper surrounding the gift. Inside was a Christmas ornament—a nativity scene carved out of delicate wood. I smiled up at him. "It's beautiful. Thank you."

He pointed to the piece. "That represents true peace on earth."

"And goodwill to men."

He hooked a hair behind my ear. "You look like you need some rest." He opened the door and paused in the doorframe as something scraped the top of his head. He reached up and pulled something green down. "Someone decorated your doorframe."

I looked up. Sure enough, someone had left mistletoe there. Now that would have been a great way to spread some Christmas cheer—leaving random bunches of mistletoe at people's houses. I'd have to remember that for next year.

I shrugged and raised my hands in innocence. "Not me."

He stared at me another moment with those mesmerizing eyes before abruptly looking away and shoving his hands into his pockets. "Look Gabby, I'm going over to a homeless shelter in the morning to give out presents. Any interest in coming?"

The chance to spend Christmas with someone other than myself? I nodded. "I'd love to."

Focusing on someone other than myself at Christmas—that seemed like the best idea ever.

I started to turn to go inside when Riley leaned down. He planted a kiss on my cheek. When he pulled back, his eyes sparkled. "Merry Christmas, Gabby St. Claire."

A grin stretched across my face. I didn't know what that kiss meant, but I did know that whether Riley was my friend or my boyfriend, I wanted to keep him around.

"Merry Christmas to you too, Riley Thomas."

###

If you enjoyed this book, you may also enjoy these Squeaky Clean Mysteries:

Hazardous Duty (Book 1)

On her way to completing a degree in forensic science, Gabby St. Claire drops out of school and starts her own crime-scene cleaning business. When a routine cleaning job uncovers a murder weapon the police overlooked, she realizes that the wrong person is in jail. But the owner of the weapon is a powerful foe . . . and willing to do anything to keep Gabby quiet. With the help of her new neighbor, Riley Thomas, a man whose life and faith fascinate her, Gabby seeks to find the killer before another murder occurs.

Suspicious Minds (Book 2)

In this smart and suspenseful sequel to *Hazardous Duty*, crime-scene cleaner Gabby St. Claire finds herself stuck doing mold remediation to pay the bills. Her first day on the job, she uncovers a surprise in the crawlspace of a dilapidated home: Elvis, dead as a doornail and still wearing his blue-suede shoes. How could she possibly keep her nose out of a case like this?

It Came Upon a Midnight Crime (Book 2.5, a Novella)

Someone is intent on destroying the true meaning of Christmas—at least, destroying anything that hints of it. All around crime-scene cleaner Gabby St. Claire's hometown, anything pointing to Jesus as "the reason for the season" is being sabotaged. The crimes become more twisted as dismembered body parts are found at the vandalisms. Someone is determined to destroy Christmas . . . but Gabby is just as determined to find the Grinch and let peace on earth and goodwill prevail.

Organized Grime (Book 3)

Gabby St. Claire knows her best friend, Sierra, isn't guilty of killing three people in what appears to be an eco-terrorist attack. But Sierra has disappeared, her only contact a frantic phone call to Gabby proclaiming she's being hunted. Gabby is determined to prove her friend is innocent and to keep Sierra alive. While trying to track down the real perpetrator, Gabby notices a disturbing trend at the crime scenes she's cleaning, one that ties random crimes together—and points to Sierra as the guilty party. Just what has her friend gotten herself involved in?

Dirty Deeds (Book 4)

"Promise me one thing. No snooping. Just for one week." Gabby St. Claire knows that her fiancé's request is a simple one she should be able to honor. After all, Riley's law school reunion and attorneys' conference at a posh resort is a chance for them to get away from the mysteries Gabby often finds herself involved in as a crime-scene cleaner. Then an old friend of Riley's goes missing. Gabby suspects one of Riley's buddies might be behind the disappearance. When the missing woman's mom asks Gabby for help, how can she say no?

The Scum of All Fears (Book 5)

Gabby St. Claire is back to crime-scene cleaning and needs help after a weekend killing spree fills her work docket. A serial killer her fiancé put behind bars has escaped. His last words to Riley were: *I'll get out, and I'll get even.* Pictures of Gabby are found in the man's prison cell, messages are left for Gabby at crime scenes, someone keeps slipping in and out of her apartment, and her temporary assistant disappears. The search for answers becomes darker when Gabby realizes she's dealing with a criminal who is truly the scum of the earth. He will do anything to make Gabby's and Riley's lives a living nightmare.

To Love, Honor, and Perish (Book 6)

Just when Gabby St. Claire's life is on the right track, the unthinkable happens. Her fiancé, Riley Thomas, is shot and in life-threatening condition only a week before their wedding. Gabby is determined to figure out who pulled the trigger, even if investigating puts her own life at risk. As she digs deeper into the case, she discovers secrets better left alone. Doubts arise in her mind, and the one man with answers lies on death's doorstep. Then an old foe returns and tests everything Gabby is made of—physically, mentally, and spiritually. Will all she's worked for be destroyed?

Mucky Streak (Book 7)

Gabby St. Claire feels her life is smeared with the stain of tragedy. She takes a short-term gig as a private investigator—a cold case that's eluded detectives for ten years. The mass murder of a wealthy family seems impossible to solve, but Gabby brings more clues to light. Add to the mix a flirtatious client, travels to an exciting new city, and some quirky—albeit temporary—new sidekicks, and things get complicated. With every new development, Gabby prays that her "mucky streak" will end and the future will become clear. Yet every answer she uncovers leads her closer to danger—both for her life and for her heart.

Foul Play (Book 8)

Gabby St. Claire is crying "foul play" in every sense of the phrase. When the crime-scene cleaner agrees to go undercover at a local community theater, she discovers more than backstage bickering, atrocious acting, and rotten writing. The female lead is dead, and an old classmate who has staked everything on the musical production's success is about to go under. In her dual role of investigator and star of the show, Gabby finds the stakes rising faster than the opening-night curtain. She must face her past and make monumental decisions, not just about the play but also concerning her future relationships and career. Will Gabby find the killer before the curtain goes down—not only on the play, but also on life as she knows it?

Broom and Gloom (Book 9)

Gabby St. Claire is determined to get back in the saddle again. While in Oklahoma for a forensic conference, she meets her soon-to-be stepbrother, Trace Ryan, an up-and-coming country singer. A woman he was dating has disappeared, and he suspects a crazy fan may be behind it. Gabby agrees to investigate, as she tries to juggle her conference, navigate being alone in a new place, and locate a woman who may not want to be found. She discovers that sometimes taking life by the horns means staring danger in the face, no matter the consequences.

Dust and Obey (Book 10)

When Gabby St. Claire's ex-fiancé, Riley Thomas, asks for her help in investigating a possible murder at a couples retreat, she knows she should say no. She knows she should run far, far away from the danger of both being around Riley and the crime. But her nosy instincts and determination take precedence over her logic. Gabby and Riley must work together to find the killer. In the process, they have to confront demons from their past and deal with their present relationship.

Thrill Squeaker (Book 11)

An abandoned theme park. An unsolved murder. A decision that will change Gabby's life forever. Restoring an old amusement park and turning it into a destination resort seems like a fun idea for former crime-scene cleaner Gabby St. Claire. The side job gives her the chance to spend time with her friends, something she's missed since beginning a new career. The job turns out to be more than Gabby bargained for when she finds a dead body on her first day. Add to the mix legends of Bigfoot, creepy clowns, and ghostlike remnants of happier times at the park, and her stay begins to feel like a rollercoaster ride. Someone doesn't want the decrepit Mythical Falls to open again, but just how far is this person willing to go to ensure this venture fails? As the stakes rise and danger creeps closer, will Gabby be able to restore things in her own life that time has destroyed—including broken relationships? Or is her future closer to the fate of the doomed Mythical Falls?

Swept Away, a Honeymoon Novella (Book 11.5)
Finding the perfect place for a honeymoon, away from any potential danger or mystery, is challenging. But Gabby's longtime love and newly minted husband, Riley Thomas, has done it. He has found a location with a nonexistent crime rate, a mostly retired population, and plenty of opportunities for relaxation in the warm sun. Within minutes of the newlyweds' arrival, a convoy of vehicles pulls up to a nearby house, and their honeymoon oasis is destroyed like a sandcastle in a storm. Despite Gabby's and Riley's determination to keep to themselves, trouble comes knocking at their door—literally—when a neighbor is abducted from the beach directly outside their rental. Will Gabby and Riley be swept away with each other during their honeymoon . . . or will a tide of danger and mayhem pull them under?

Cunning Attractions **(Book 12)**
Coming soon

***While You Were Sweeping*, a Riley Thomas Novella**
Riley Thomas is trying to come to terms with life after a traumatic brain injury turned his world upside down. Away from everything familiar—including his crime-scene-cleaning former fiancée and his career as a social-rights attorney—he's determined to prove himself and regain his old life. But when he claims he witnessed his neighbor shoot and kill someone, everyone thinks he's crazy. When all evidence of the crime disappears, even Riley has to wonder if he's losing his mind.

Note: *While You Were Sweeping* is a spin-off mystery written in conjunction with the Squeaky Clean series featuring crime-scene cleaner Gabby St. Claire.

The Sierra Files:

Pounced (Book 1)
Animal-rights activist Sierra Nakamura never expected to stumble upon the dead body of a coworker while filming a project nor get involved in the investigation. But when someone threatens to kill her cats unless she hands over the "information," she becomes more bristly than an angry feline. Making matters worse is the fact that her cats—and the investigation—are driving a wedge between her and her boyfriend, Chad. With every answer she uncovers, old hurts rise to the surface and test her beliefs. Saving her cats might mean ruining everything else in her life. In the fight for survival, one thing is certain: either pounce or be pounced.

Hunted (Book 2)
Who knew a stray dog could cause so much trouble? Newlywed animal-rights activist Sierra Nakamura Davis must face her worst nightmare: breaking the news she eloped with Chad to her ultra-opinionated tiger mom. Her perfectionist parents have planned a vow-renewal ceremony at Sierra's lush childhood home, but a neighborhood dog ruins the rehearsal dinner when it shows up toting what appears to be a fresh human bone.

While dealing with the dog, a nosy neighbor, and an old flame turning up at the wrong times, Sierra hunts for answers. Her journey of discovery leads to more than just who committed the crime.

Pranced (Book 2.5, a Christmas novella)

Sierra Nakamura Davis thinks spending Christmas with her husband's relatives will be a real Yuletide treat. But when the animal-rights activist learns his family has a reindeer farm, she begins to feel more like the Grinch. Even worse, when Sierra arrives, she discovers the reindeer are missing. Sierra fears the animals might be suffering a worse fate than being used for entertainment purposes. Can Sierra set aside her dogmatic opinions to help get the reindeer home in time for the holidays? Or will secrets tear the family apart and ruin Sierra's dream of the perfect Christmas?

Rattled (Book 3)

"What do you mean a thirteen-foot lavender albino ball python is missing?" Tough-as-nails Sierra Nakamura Davis isn't one to get flustered. But trying to balance being a wife and a new mom with her crusade to help animals is proving harder than she imagined. Add a missing python, a high maintenance intern, and a dead body to the mix, and Sierra becomes the definition of rattled. Can

she balance it all—and solve a possible murder—
without losing her mind?

Holly Anna Paladin Mysteries:

Random Acts of Murder (Book 1)

When Holly Anna Paladin is given a year to live, she embraces her final days doing what she loves most—random acts of kindness. But one of her extreme good deeds goes horribly wrong, implicating her in a string of murders. Holly is suddenly thrust into a different kind of fight for her life. Could it also be random that the detective assigned to the case is her old high school crush and present-day nemesis? Will Holly find the killer before he ruins what is left of her life? Or will she spend her final days alone and behind bars?

Random Acts of Deceit (Book 2)

"Break up with Chase Dexter, or I'll kill him." Holly Anna Paladin never expected such a gut-wrenching ultimatum. With home invasions, hidden cameras, and bomb threats, Holly must make some serious choices. Whatever she decides, the consequences will either break her heart or break her soul. She tries to match wits with the Shadow Man, but the more she fights, the deeper she's drawn into the perilous situation. With her sister's wedding problems and the riots in the city, Holly has nearly reached her breaking point. She must stop this mystery man before someone she loves dies. But the deceit is threatening to pull her under . . . six feet under.

Random Acts of Malice (Book 3)

When Holly Anna Paladin's boyfriend, police detective Chase Dexter, says he's leaving for two weeks and can't give any details, she wants to trust him. But when she discovers Chase may be involved in some unwise and dangerous pursuits, she's compelled to intervene. Holly gets a run for her money as she's swept into the world of horseracing. The stakes turn deadly when a dead body surfaces and suspicion is cast on Chase. At every turn, more trouble emerges, making Holly question what she holds true about her relationship and her future. Just when she thinks she's on the homestretch, a dark horse arises. Holly might lose everything in a nail-biting fight to the finish.

Random Acts of Scrooge (Book 3.5)

Christmas is supposed to be the most wonderful time of the year, but a real-life Scrooge is threatening to ruin the season's good will. Holly Anna Paladin can't wait to celebrate Christmas with family and friends. She loves everything about the season—celebrating the birth of Jesus, singing carols, and baking Christmas treats, just to name a few. But when a local family needs help, how can she say no? Holly's community has come together to help raise funds to save the home of Greg and Babette Sullivan, but a Bah-Humburgler has snatched the canisters of cash. Holly and her boyfriend, police detective Chase Dexter, team up to catch the Christmas crook. Will they succeed in collecting enough cash to cover the Sullivans' overdue bills? Or will someone succeed in ruining Christmas for all those involved?

Random Acts of Greed (Book 4)

Help me. Don't trust anyone. Do-gooder Holly Anna Paladin can't believe her eyes when a healthy baby boy is left on her doorstep. What seems like good fortune quickly turns into concern when blood spatter is found on the bottom of the baby carrier. Something tragic—maybe deadly—happened in connection with the infant. The note left only adds to the confusion. What does it mean by "Don't trust anyone"? Holly is determined to figure out the identity of the baby. Is his mom someone from the youth center where she volunteers? Or maybe the connection is through Holly's former job as a social worker? Even worse—what if the blood belongs to the baby's mom? Every answer Holly uncovers only leads to more questions. A sticky web of intrigue captures her imagination until she's sure of only one thing: she must protect the baby at all cost.

Carolina Moon Series:

Home Before Dark (Book 1)
Nothing good ever happens after dark. Country singer Daleigh McDermott's father often repeated those words. Now, her father is dead. As she's about to flee back to Nashville, she finds his hidden journal with hints that his death was no accident. Mechanic Ryan Shields is the only one who seems to believe Daleigh. Her father trusted the man, but her attraction to Ryan scares her. She knows her life and career are back in Nashville and her time in the sleepy North Carolina town is only temporary. As Daleigh and Ryan work to unravel the mystery, it becomes obvious that someone wants them dead. They must rely on each other—and on God—if they hope to make it home before the darkness swallows them.

Gone By Dark (Book 2)
Ten years ago, Charity White's best friend, Andrea, was abducted as they walked home from school. A decade later, when Charity receives a mysterious letter that promises answers, she returns to North Carolina in search of closure. With the help of her new neighbor, Police Officer Joshua Haven, Charity begins to track down mysterious clues concerning her friend's abduction. They soon discover that

they must work together or both of them will be swallowed by the looming darkness.

Wait Until Dark (Book 3)

A woman grieving broken dreams. A man struggling to regain memories. A secret entrenched in folklore dating back two centuries. Antiquarian Felicity French has no clue the trouble she's inviting in when she rescues a man outside her grandma's old plantation house during a treacherous snowstorm. All she wants is to nurse her battered heart and wounded ego, as well as come to terms with her past. Now she's stuck inside with a stranger sporting an old bullet wound and forgotten hours. Coast Guardsman Brody Joyner can't remember why he was out in such perilous weather, how he injured his head, or how a strange key got into his pocket. Brody and Felicity's rocky start goes from tense to worse when danger closes in. Who else wants the mysterious key that somehow ended up in Brody's pocket? Why? The unlikely duo quickly becomes entrenched in an adventure of a lifetime, one that could have ties to local folklore and Felicity's ancestors. But sometimes the past leads to darkness . . . darkness that doesn't wait for anyone.

Cape Thomas Series:

Dubiosity (Book 1)
Savannah Harris vowed to leave behind her old life as an investigative reporter. But when two migrant workers go missing, her curiosity spikes. As more eerie incidents begin afflicting the area, each works to draw Savannah out of her seclusion and raise the stakes—for her and the surrounding community. Even as Savannah's new boarder, Clive Miller, makes her feel things she thought long forgotten, she suspects he's hiding something too, and he's not the only one. As secrets emerge and danger closes in, Savannah must choose between faith and uncertainty. One wrong decision might spell the end . . . not just for her but for everyone around her. Will she unravel the mystery in time, or will doubt get the best of her?

Disillusioned (Book 2)
Nikki Wright is desperate to help her brother, Bobby, who hasn't been the same since escaping from a detainment camp run by terrorists in Colombia. Rumor has it that he betrayed his navy brothers and conspired with those who held him hostage, and both the press and the military are hounding him for answers. All Nikki wants is to shield her brother so he has time to recover and

heal. But soon they realize the paparazzi are the least of their worries. When a group of men try to abduct Nikki and her brother, Bobby insists that Kade Wheaton, another former SEAL, can keep them out of harm's way. But can Nikki trust Kade? After all, the man who broke her heart eight years ago is anything but safe...Hiding out in a farmhouse on the Chesapeake Bay, Nikki finds her loyalties—and the remnants of her long-held faith—tested as she and Kade put aside their differences to keep Bobby's increasingly erratic behavior under wraps. But when Bobby disappears, Nikki will have to trust Kade completely if she wants to uncover the truth about a rumored conspiracy. Nikki's life—and the fate of the nation—depends on it.

Standalones:

The Good Girl

Tara Lancaster can sing "Amazing Grace" in three harmonies, two languages, and interpret it for the hearing impaired. She can list the Bible canon backward, forward, and alphabetized. The only time she ever missed church was when she had pneumonia and her mom made her stay home. Then her life shatters and her reputation is left in ruins. She flees halfway across the country to dog-sit, but the quiet anonymity she needs isn't waiting at her sister's house. Instead, she finds a knife with a threatening message, a fame-hungry friend, a too-hunky neighbor, and evidence of . . . a ghost? Following all the rules has gotten her nowhere. And nothing she learned in Sunday School can tell her where to go from there.

Death of the Couch Potato's Wife (Suburban Sleuth Mysteries)

You haven't seen desperate until you've met Laura Berry, a career-oriented city slicker turned suburbanite housewife. Well-trained in the big-city commandment, "mind your own business," Laura is persuaded by her spunky seventy-year-old neighbor, Babe, to check on another neighbor who hasn't been seen in days. She finds Candace Flynn, wife of the infamous "Couch King," dead, and at last has a reason to get up in the morning. Someone is determined to stop her from digging deeper into the death of her neighbor, but Laura is just as determined to figure out who is behind the death-by-poisoned-pork-rinds.

Imperfect

Since the death of her fiancé two years ago, novelist Morgan Blake's life has been in a holding pattern. She has a major case of writer's block, and a book signing in the mountain town of Perfect sounds as perfect as its name. Her trip takes a wrong turn when she's involved in a hit-and-run: She hit a man, and he ran from the scene. Before fleeing, he mouthed the word "Help." First she must find him. In Perfect, she finds a small town that offers all she ever wanted. But is something sinister going on behind its cheery exterior? Was she invited as a guest of honor simply to do a book signing? Or was she lured to town for another purpose—a deadly purpose?

The Gabby St. Claire Diaries:
a tween mystery series

The Curtain Call Caper (Book 1)

Is a ghost haunting the Oceanside Middle School auditorium? What else could explain the disasters surrounding the play—everything from missing scripts to a falling spotlight and damaged props? Seventh-grader Gabby St. Claire has dreamed about being part of her school's musical, but a series of unfortunate events threatens to shut down the production. While trying to uncover the culprit and save her fifteen minutes of fame, she also has to manage impossible teachers, cliques, her dysfunctional family, and a secret she can't tell even her best friend. Will Gabby figure out who or what is sabotaging the show . . . or will it be curtains for her and the rest of the cast?

The Disappearing Dog Dilemma (Book 2)

Why are dogs disappearing around town? When two friends ask seventh-grader Gabby St. Claire for her help in finding their missing canines, Gabby decides to unleash her sleuthing skills to sniff out whoever is behind the act. But time management and relationships get tricky as worrisome weather, a part-time job, and a new crush interfere with Gabby's investigation. Will her determination crack the case? Or will shadowy villains, a penchant for overcommitting, and even her own heart put her in the doghouse?

The Bungled Bike Burglaries (Book 3)

Stolen bikes and a long-forgotten time capsule leave one amateur sleuth baffled and busy. Seventh-grader Gabby St. Claire is determined to bring a bike burglar to justice—and not just because mean girl Donabell Bullock is strong-arming her. But each new clue brings its own set of trouble. As if that's not enough, Gabby finds evidence of a decades-old murder within the contents of the time capsule, but no one seems to take her seriously. As her investigation heats up, will Gabby's knack for being in the wrong place at the wrong time with the wrong people crack the case? Or will it prove hazardous to her health?

Complete Book List:

Squeaky Clean Mysteries:
#1 Hazardous Duty
#2 Suspicious Minds
#2.5 It Came Upon a Midnight Crime (a novella)
#3 Organized Grime
#4 Dirty Deeds
#5 The Scum of All Fears
#6 To Love, Honor, and Perish
#7 Mucky Streak
#8 Foul Play
#9 Broom and Gloom
#10 Dust and Obey
#11 Thrill Squeaker
#11.5 Swept Away (a novella)
#12 Cunning Attractions (coming soon)

Squeaky Clean Companion Novella:
While You Were Sweeping

The Sierra Files:
#1 Pounced
#2 Hunted
#2.5 Pranced (a Christmas novella)
#3 Rattled
#4 Caged (coming soon)

The Gabby St. Claire Diaries (a Tween Mystery series):
#1 The Curtain Call Caper
#2 The Disappearing Dog Dilemma
#3 The Bungled Bike Burglaries

Holly Anna Paladin Mysteries:
#1 Random Acts of Murder
#2 Random Acts of Deceit
#3 Random Acts of Malice
#3.5 Random Acts of Scrooge
#4 Random Acts of Greed
#5 Random Acts of Fraud (coming soon)

Carolina Moon Series:
Home Before Dark
Gone By Dark
Wait Until Dark

Suburban Sleuth Mysteries:
#1 Death of the Couch Potato's Wife

Stand-alone Romantic-Suspense:
Keeping Guard
The Last Target
Race Against Time
Ricochet
Key Witness

Lifeline
High-Stakes Holiday Reunion
Desperate Measures
Hidden Agenda
Mountain Hideaway
Dark Harbor
Shadow of Suspicion (coming soon)

Cape Thomas Series:
Dubiosity
Disillusioned
Distorted (coming in 2017)

Standalone Romantic Mystery:
The Good Girl

Suspense:
Imperfect

Nonfiction:
Changed: True Stories of Finding God through
Christian Music
The Novel in Me: The Beginner's Guide to Writing
and Publishing a Novel

Made in the USA
Middletown, DE
03 December 2019